Contents

Conflict on Earths

Introduction

In the near future, not so far from nowadays, the whole world on the earth will be full of wars, and poverty will spread out to reach every the whole world, the resources of earth will decrease because of the increased number of population. Life on earth will be unbearable and people will starve to death. Each person on earth will be completely despair and waiting for his doom. All solutions are in vain except finding another place to live; suddenly a very old satellite sends signals that indicate existence of water on a planet near our galaxy. Unexpectedly, the new impulse of hope comes to each heart. They donated to dispense with their rights in gas and oil to complete the project of leaving the earth to live in a better place.

The project starts and the first regiment of human traveled to the new land which is supposed to be full of treasures. What will they find? Will they find what they had dreamed of? Will the new land be full of welfares as they thought? Will it be easy to occupy another planet in another galaxy?

At first, they thought that they will not face any difficulties in dominating this land, but when they reached there, they discovered the reality. Will they continue the project? No way else.

So what will they do...?

Chapter1

Once upon a time there was something called Earth treasures, but now in our world, on our earth, living standards had reached the maximum limit. Unemployment rate is rising every minute, there are lot of crimes. Oil had risen up to the highest price because many wells had stopped production. People consumed all resources on earth, groundwater wells, gold, gas and oil. In Arabian Gulf zone, oil decreased dramatically. The biggest oil field in the world closed its doors after its resources had finished. Scientists decided that oil in Arabian Gulf area, especially in Saudi Arabia, will be sufficient for only the coming 50 years. All over the past years, people had consumed all resources of earth crops, animals, metals, even oxygen. There was Chaos all over the world like upheavals against Kings and presidents, wars almost break out between big countries like America, Russia, and China because of the economic crisis. China became the biggest economic power controlling the world followed by Russia in the second place because of arms trade business.

The world's scientists had decided that they must find a solution. Professor (Michel de Silva) had an idea, He suggested that people move to another planet, which is called (the new earth) where people can reproduce and transfer science.

There is a planet similar to our planet earth in geographical land marks and the existence of water, but it is far from earth about 35 years long by a spacecraft according to minimum science estimations.

Scientists were facing a big problem. If they send a 25 or 30 old person, he may die before reaching the new planet, and that is why United States had decided to send 15 years old heroes and train them well to save the world.

Scientists had designed an aircraft, which can work for 65 years by nuclear energy, to discover the planet (new-earth). The mission is sending a small rocket to the planet earth when they arrive to the new planet, and to send signals to confirm the scientific theory that there is existence of water and life on the new-earth, and then scientists shall send young people and their families to start a new prosperity life.

United States announced the world that the project is starting, and if anyone wants to volunteer will be welcomed to perpetuate his name forever. Moreover, participant's parents shall receive 5 million dollars provided that participant's age shall not exceed 15 years old, and he shall pass the IQ exam.

5 persons applied to participate, two of them did not pass the IQ exam, and the remaining three were accepted. Some people considered it a big risk, which has success rate only 10% not more. They may live or die. People were not convinced. United States honored all the volunteers. And the president of the United States expressed his eagerness and happiness because Americans shall save the world and the United States' flag will be waving high on the new-earth planet.

The first one is (André), 11 years old, son of an army's officer. His mother did not accept the idea. However, his father had insisted to respond to nation's call.

The second one is (Ricardo), 14 years old. His mother abandoned him while he was a baby. He was brought up by his uncle. Ricardo is Mexican, whose father is in an American prison as he is spending a life sentence because of drug and smuggling.

5

The third one is (Vallen), 15 years old. An African American boy. His parents decided to send him because of poverty, so that the family gains enough money for living.

(Swariz Adriano), 59years old, decided to voluntarily go with the children and train them to use the spacecraft, until he dies. He is an obsessed with space and loves to travel through it.

The three were trained on using the spacecraft devices and what to do in emergency. Training them was difficult as they were young, considering that any fault may cost them their lives. They were trained in NASA on spacecraft simulators. And they improved within six months.
(Thomas)Their trainer, said that these simulators are not real, It may not be very much like the real situation and if any problem occurred you have to solve it by yourselves you shall avoid any fault. We will be contacting you in case of any problem; however, such communication will not last for long time because satellites shall not go more far than its orbits, and this may end the communication between us at any moment. "You shall revise guidelines and instructions books of the spacecraft in case of any problem or defection he said. You will be drinking water from the water -cycling device and taking pills that scientists invented to provide energy and proteins to keep you alive, the course is 3 pills are enough, These pills prevent hunger and man can live on for lifetime. Spacecraft was provided by huge amounts of these pills to keep them alive for at least 56 years.

Heroes are ready

Heroes were provided by essential educational books. They were instructed to make benefit of their time by reading these books which were about 450 books in all science, physics, mathematics, etc.

Great crowdedness of people from all over the world was present. Satellite channels were ready to broadcast this unique new event. The world witnessed the farewell ceremony of the heroes: André, Ricardo, Vallen and their leader Swarize. Also some presidents and kings from all over the world attended this important ceremony.

Heroes were saluted; their families were honored by given Honorary Medal from the US President, then they entered the spacecraft with tears in their eyes, as they were going to leave behind their families for a lifetime. The whole world was clapping hardly even those in front of TVs.

National anthem was played and the whole world was watching. Count down began. They interred the spacecraft at NASA.

Countdown begins and The spacecraft started the journey; the world was watching the 3 heroes Andre, Recardo and Vallen, praying to god everywhere to save them so that they save the world.

NASA was contacting them, reassure them that the spacecraft is ok, and all devices were working properly.

Two months later. Communication between spacecraft and earth was cut. They felt a little bit annoyed, as they should not be able to hear any voice from earth after that.

9 years passed. They were working hard and they arranged spacecraft controlling among them by a schedule, so that each of them take a rest for 8 hours.

They learned everything. In this regard, Thanks to Swarize their leader and father. He was teaching them everything. However, Swarize died at 68 years old. He died in his bed. André, Ricardo and Vallen cried him as if he was their real father.
It was his wish to live and die in space, moving freely between planets.
They prayed for him and sent him out of the craft in space.

Time passed. Andre liked reading in his spare time, so that he could make benefit and learn.
Ricardo and Vallen liked to play with IPad, listen to music, dance and play in their spare time.
Sometimes they were entering André's room, take his books and through them on the floor. "Come on André, let's play." they said while they were laughing. "You have plenty of time to read it 100 times." He used to play with them a little then he went back again to read his educational books.

One day it was Vallen's turn in the control room. Andre entered the room. "I am going to sleep," said André. "I am so tired that I cannot sit with you. Please take care of the control. I shall have some rest". When it is Vallen's turn to take control, he gets angry, as he liked to play and sleep. A quarrel usually rises between him, André and Austin, because he doesn't like to stay alone in the control room.

Control room was equipped by the latest devices and sensors. There was a developed radar to give any alert against any strange body near the spacecraft.

It was Vallen's turn. Andre and Austin were sleeping. Vallen was feeling bored while monitoring. He played music on the iPod.. He put on earphones until he fell asleep. Spacecraft was moving without manual control. Suddenly computers gave a strong alarm that there was a body in front of the spacecraft. Vallen was listening to the alarm as if it is a dream. He dreamed that he was playing in a fun fair and listening to games sounds. Then he opened his eyes and began to realize everything. He saw alarm lights flashing and heard alarms. He woke up and took the steering control of the spacecraft and he put down the earphones, he saw a huge rook in front of him. He pulled steering wheel up, away from the huge rock. The Huge rock was about to bump into the front of the spacecraft. However, it hit the craft's back from beneath.

The sound was strong. Both André and Ricardo woke up in horror. Alarm devices were beeping continuously. "What is happening? What is happening?" Both of them hurried to the control room.
"What happens? " Ricardo and André asked.
"I am sorry.."Vallen answered while he was crying and trembling
"What happened? Speak up." said André.
Vallen said, I fall asleep, and when I woke up I saw a huge rock in front of me and I couldn't do anything except raising the ship up so I can avoid collision, But I heard the explosion".
Andre inspected the computer, the alert was from gases inside the spacecraft, low pressure and oxygen began to decrees. Andre and Ricardo went to inspect damages in the craft. There was a hole at the back of the craft. The hole was not big, but pressure goes low and gases were entering inside the craft. They inspected the craft, it was working well. They returned to the craft in order to put a plan. At the control cabinet Vallen stood up. "This happened because of you. You left me alone and nothing was amusing me. Said Vallen.

Ricardo hit Vallen and they both fell on the ground. Vallen hit Recardo's hands with the fire extinguisher. "Stop it. Stop it." said André. We have no time for fighting. If we did not solve the problem, we would die. Please stop this now, we have to solve the problem." Ricardo was holding his hands anguished. "Ricardo, are you ok?" asked André. "Yes, I am ok," answered Ricardo. "But I still feel some pain."

Vallen went to his bed mewling feeling sorry for what he did. "God dame my family, why did they send me here? To die for sure." Vallen said while he was weeping.

Andre brought a bandage and tied Ricardo's hands. They were working hardly to fix the damage.

Andre decided to go and open orifice that leads to the back of the craft. There was a lot of noise as well as a strong cracking sound from the low pressure.

Andre returned to the cabinet. "We need Vallen."Said André to Ricardo, then he went to Vallen's room. Vallen was still weeping. He hugged Andre and apologized for what happened. "I didn't mean to put you down but I felt sleep." said Vallen. "It's ok. Forget it. We have work to do. Now, please take control of the craft while we fix the problem." Replied André "We have a big job to do".

They went together to the cabinet and found Ricardo taking control.

"I am sorry, brother. I was not conscious and I didn't mean to hit you," said Ricardo.

He was crying. "I don't want to die at early age." said Vallen. Ricardo hugged him and apologized, as he was the one who began quarreling and hitting.

"We are here like brothers," said Ricardo. "Things like this always happen between brothers. They always quarrel then they reconcile".

They decided to go and fix the whole existed beneath the craft by welding this hole. "Vallin please sit here and take control," said Ricardo. "We shall carry out the mission".

"No" said André "your hand is still injured and you will not be able to hold iron strongly. Valien, please come with me." They took some iron panels and welding wires and went on their way.

They opened the orifice, went down stairs, and closed ceiling opening. The pressure was very law. It is very hard working in such circumstances. He put an iron panel but he could not fix it. It was very hard because there is no gravity. Vallen asked André to allow him to go to Ricardo to decrease craft's speed, so that they might be able to weld the craft. But once André went upstairs, suddenly, a part of the floor where Vallen was standing on had cracked. It took only a few minutes then Vallen disappeared. Andre caught the stairs and screamed "Vallen" "Ricardo, help me". He was crying and calling Ricardo who couldn't hear him due to laud alarm sounds. He couldn't save his colleague after he tried hard, he went upstairs. And sat down and began to cry. Andre went to Ricardo in the control room. "What happened?" asked Ricardo. "Vallen died" André answered. Ricardo grieved him too.

They were both sitting in the driving cabinet. Alarm sets were working. Computer was warning decrease of oxygen rates from 100% to 75%. It was decreasing 1%per hour.

They were both waiting death.

"We have no choice, whether to live or to die. "Said André " it was a big mistake that we haven't read the guidance book".

Andre went quickly to bring the emergency guidance book and they followed the instructions:

1- *To decrease craft's speed by 50%*
2- *To tie rob around your back and hang to the ceiling.*
3- *Prepare needed iron panel.*

4- Prepare welding wire, and then connect to power supply.

5- Oxygen and clothes.

He went quickly to prepare needed tools. He prepared rob, iron panel, welding wires, oxygen and the space suite which he left at descending place.

He returned to the control room to take the right time and to be sure that there are no rocks or bodies nearby the craft. The radar did not determine any bodies nearby. They decreased the speed and went quickly to tie them self with robs then hang robs up so that they shall not swim around while welding. They wear the space suits and went down. Outer space seen was terrifying. Andre took iron panel and put on damage's place. Then Ricardo welded the whole and the missing parts.

They went back quickly to the control cabinet. GOD providence saved their lives from any crashes, due to existence of modern radar. They knew that they have mistaken by not reading the guidance. They collected Vallen's stuff in a box as a memory.

Years passed, and they grow up. Their friendship and brotherhood became closed too.

They were working hard and celebrating Vallen's memory annually, by standing in front of the hole and pray for him.

Days and years passed, they are near the new planet the dream is about to come true. They were thinking only about reaching the new land.

The craft was working well. After about one year and 9 months, they were one month far from reaching the new land. Andre was 41 years old and Ricardo was 44 years old. Ready to go down.

New land

The new land was ruled by a cruel king, named Walter. He had a huge, great empire with very high walls. Such walls were high that nobody can easily pass. The king had an invincible high-trained army, with high standard in fighting, protecting and physical force. Such army's individuals were carefully selected.

The king had one daughter called Kathen, and a wife called Suzan.

Main worship in the empire was related to the god (Flying Serpent). It was a statue in the temple with a shape of Copra snake, standing at full length, with two wings, opening his mouth and showing his tongue. People there believed that it protected them and poisoned anyone who tried to attack them. In the temple, all people of the empire prayed, offered food, wine, presents, eucharis for this statue every year.

There was a priestess called (Tessa), 27 years old. She inherited her magic powers from her late mother. Before she died, Tessa's mother told her that "if the last day of the year is corresponding to Saturday, then prepare eucharis for the statue, and read the books under your hand. Demons and elves shall tell you only one buried matter, whether good or evil. If evil, they shall tell you how to get rid of that evil. If good, you must offer them what they demand so that they shall be dissatisfied with you".

On that year, Saturday was the last day of the year. Tessa took a chicken and made eucharis in the temple at night. She was told that a star shall fall from the sky and that the person riding this star shall destroy the empire, the king, and the people and destroy god's statue as well.

She was frightened and went to meet King Walter. She told the guards that she must meet the king at once. They did not allow here to enter because King Walter hated her and hated her mother, too. He was looking at them as if he was seeing a devil. Guards drove her away. While she was returning, she saw Eric going to the palace.

Eric was King's cousin, a member of senates, who was in love with the priestess (Tessa). He used to believe in her and to give her money so that she tell him about his future and his life. Most of her words were true. He was in love with her, and they both were having an intimate relationship. "I want to meet the king for an emergency," said Tessa to Eric. "It is important, and it is related to my life, your life and the empire."Eric got worried. "Ok" Eric said, "Wait here". He went to meet King Walter, and then the King gave her permission for a meeting. "Your majesty"said Tessa to the king, "I knew that a star shall fall down from the sky upon which a person may be riding. Such person shall work on destroying our god, our life, our empire and us. There is a condition to stop this star."The king laughed at her words. "How could anybody destroy the most powerful empire in the whole universe?"Said the King. "Do you know that more than 200 thousand persons died beneath our empire's walls? They could not penetrate these walls. And you are talking about one person??!!!!". "I just told you what shall happen," replied the priestess. "If you seek safety for yourself, your family, your women, your men and your god you must accept god's condition. There is no time to lose."
Then she went away.

King Walter said to Eric "do you believe this crazy woman? She is just a priestess. No sensible man can believe her. How could any man overcome an empire, which lasted for thousands of years? How can such man overcome its Impenetrable

Fortress? Its strong men? How could such man make a strong King like me to fall down?"

"I believe her, your majesty," said Eric. "She did not lie to us before. I am anxious about this matter. Senates shall meet tomorrow and take votes." The king refused to listen to this crazy priestess. Eric insisted to hold an urgent meeting to the senates by the next day. Senates are a council formed of empire's scientists and seniors of the state. They are King Walter's cousins.

On the meeting date, some members objected the priestess. On the other hand, some members believed in her words. The king refused to attend the meeting because he considered this matter as a silly one, which did not need to be discussed in a meeting of senior senates. The senates considered this matter as threaten to their home nation. They refused to mocks any issue, which is related to their empire's interest even if it did not matter the king.

The king was annoyed due to senate's decision, who decided to agree with the priestess's condition. A messenger was sent to tell the priestess that the condition has been accepted. Besides, to tell her to attend before the king on the next day to tell about the condition to avoid the coming star, which threatened king's life and the empire.

When the priestess came, a close and very confidential meeting was held. King Walter was shaking his leg on the ground. Senate's members were listing to the priestess and to her demands. She was looking to King's eyes directly. "What is the condition?" asked the king. "God asks for eucharis of three virgin girls, without any injury or harm. They must be new reached puberty did not exceed more than a year "said Tessa. King left his chair and annoyed from this condition. "Why three girls?" asked the king. "Isn't one girl enough for your god?".

"God seeks power from such eucharis" The priestess replied "so that it may be able to stop the star before destroying our planet. It is very very near, and he shall fight you alone." The king stood up angrily and slapped her. "Shut your mouth up" the King shouted at her. "Are you here to tell me that one of my men who can kill 10 persons may be defeated by only one person? We heard your words you fool. Now, get out of here before I give my orders to crucify you." "Don't be late" said the priestess while she was going out. "Eucharis must be offered this month. You have only 3 weeks from today. He is coming, he is coming". People were looking at her and she was looking at people. She stuck to each person of sarong and say:"he is coming very soon I can see your bodies on the ground, your bodies will be eaten by vultures and crows".

The king did not speak for a while. The senate was berserk. Some members were agreeing with the priestess's words. Some others were objecting here. Senates were arguing with the king. Babel, senior senate, and a wise scientist, stood up and said "listen to me, what shall happen when we offer three virgins to god? It has never been disappointing to us. It protects us; provide us victory on our enemies. Perhaps she is right and if we disobeyed her we shall lose."

"Ok." Said the king "do what you want, but under one condition. If the priestess is proved to be a liar I shall cut her head and crucify her."

Senates decided to listen to the priestess's orders, seeking for great empire's safety and security.

The king sends four men and an odalisque to look for three girls at hill's village.

Hill's Village

A village occupied by old men and War amputees. Those who lost part of their bodies, or lost their minds. Even those who gained infectious diseases were sent to this village. Their leader was called (Yamen), 55 years old; he was the one who put village's rules. He was village's wise man.

The King used to send one of his odalisques, named Emma, and some soldiers to bring servants to the king. If the king liked the servant then she might stay and if the king did not like the servant, then she might go back to the village, or the king might give her to any of his friends.

The village was a castaway one. It was not included in empire's guards. The king considered villagers as dead. He was leaving them without any care or food. Even hunting was prohibited to those villagers. Hunting was one of king's rights. Those who violated such prohibition were crucified. Villagers depended on agriculture. In winter, villagers were starving. Some of king's servants smuggled food to their families. Servants who were discovered doing this were executed. The king considered this village as useless within the society and the empire.

Searching for Girls

King's soldiers entered the village and found no one with the same features except an orphan girl who was living with her old grandmother. They took the girl to the palace and put her in a room where no one could enter so that she might not know about the matter.

The king ordered to search. For a new virgin girl, every girl was inspected. But they didn't find except two girls.

A blacksmith named (Kommar) was having a lonely girl whose mother died at her birth. He loved his daughter very much as he was not gifted but her. She did not use to go outdoors without his permission, and he was working hard to earn his and his daughter's living.
He was one of the cleverest blacksmiths in the village. He was making solid swords and armors to the king and soldiers.

Soldiers entered his house. Odalisques inspect the girl and found out that she met all specifications needed. They took her by force. Blacksmith resisted the soldiers but they defeated him as they raised their swords to him. They was about to kill him. (Leave her, take me instead of her, I have no children but her) he shouted (why does the king want to take my child).
(Kommar), the blacksmith went to meet the king.
(Your Majesty, I am an old man and no one help me except my daughter. I have no children but her)said the blacksmith to the king. "Please give her back to me. You do not need her. She is a small girl and understands nothing". He went to kiss king's feet. "Would you sell me your daughter?" asked the king. Blacksmith was astonished.
"Your Majesty" said the blacksmith "my daughter is not for sale even if I receive gold equals to her weight".
"If you do not agree to sell her to me I shall take her by force." Said the king, brought out money and throw to the blacksmith.

"This is your daughter's value," said the king "if she worked for her lifetime she would not be able to receive this amount of money. Now, take your money, go back to your work and forget about your daughter."

Blacksmith went out broken hearted for his only daughter who did not know anyone but him crying for her. The king sends a guard to follow blacksmith with money. Blacksmith begged the guard to take the money and to help him to take his daughter back the guard looked at him silently while his eyes were saying I wish I can help you then he turned silently and went back.

Blacksmith throw the money away. Money fallen on the ground and people gathered to collect. Blacksmith's daughter was crying and shouting, "Daddy, I want my daddy". She did not know why she was in this place. Besides, there was the orphan girl crying for her grandmother.

The King appointed guards on the girls. Nobody entered to both girls but an odalisque to offer them food.

Only one girl remained. Search took place all over the city to search for this girl with such qualifications. However, it was useless.

Every Saturday, the king met senates. Most discussions were going around the last girl. More than a member suggested sending5 caravans from the army to search for the last girl.

One day the king gifted his daughter Kathen, of 14 years old, a small wooden horse. He put his gift beside her bed. She liked horses very much, dreaming to be a knight, aiming to be successor for her father. Eric was sitting alone with the king to discuss with him necessity of finalizing last girl's matter, and to persuade him to send his men to search for the girl overseas as there is no enough time. Only two weeks remained for eucharis date. Suddenly King's daughter Kathen opened the door and ran to hug her father the king and thank him for his gift. "I have nobody dearer than you" said the king.

Eric went to the priestess and said:" I have some news for you but I am not sure yet. I found the third girl". "Where and who is she?" asked Tessa

"Kathen, King's daughter" said Eric. "But I don't know whether she is adult or not".

Even if she is adult, do you think that the king shall accept to sacrifice his daughter as eucharis to god?"."If he did not accept we shall enforce him," said Eric. "Our lives and our children's lives are more important than his daughter. I shall not stand silent".

Searching for third girl was going on, while people did not know what is going on. For the first time within king's era, the king search for something in such way. Every one asked what is going on?.

One week before eucharis date there was an urgent meeting between senates and the king.

"Call the priestess," said the king. "She may find us some solution"

The priestess came. The king said to her: "we found only two girls. We did not find third girl."

"On contrary your majesty". Said the priestess "the third girl exists and I know her". The king and senates were astonished to her so. "Who is she?"Asked the king "send somebody to bring her here". The priestess said: "I am afraid to make you angry".

"Why shall I be angry with you?"Asked the king. The priestess was stammering. "Speak up" said the king. "Third girl shall be your daughter "replied the priestess. The king stood up angrily and slapped the priestess. "Guards, take her to prison," the king said then he added "meeting is over".

The king went out angrily. He went to his wife, Suzan, who asked the king "why are you angry?". "Nothing, just simple conflict" replied the king.

Before specified date, they met again.

"Search took place all over empire, even in the village soldiers did not find anything," said the king. "I hope her words shall not be correct to crucify her."

They tried to persuade the king to release the priestess but the king refused. "She shall remain in prison". "I wish if I have a daughter," said Eric."I would have sacrificed her for our god immediately".

"What do you mean by this, Eric?"Asked the king

"I mean nothing, it is just a wish". Eric replied, "Anyone is free to wish anything."

"Is there anything else than the priestess matter?" asked the king.

There was no answer, and meeting was over.

In the evening, they heard a strong sound. Some people saw something looked like a star falling over the empire. Then they heard something hitting the ground. King jumped up from his chair. Some members of senate came to the king.

"Your Majesty, did you hear that sound?"Senates said. One of the members said "I saw something looking like a star falling from the sky. It was close and clear sound then it hit the ground."

The king was worry and afraid. He ordered the guards to go and search everywhere.

Guards went out and searched but they found nothing.

Tessa, in her prison was laughing. "Welcome to your new home" said Tessa. The king called the priestess. "Is there any solution?" the king asked the priestess. "Yes" answered the priestess "your daughter".

"Send her back to prison" said the king" torture her but keep her alive".

Landing on the new Earth

Andre and Recardo lost consciousness after ship colliding with earth. They fell in a small lake between oak trees. Andre woke up at birds tweet and sound of water fall. Not knowing at first where he was and what has happened, he gradually started to regain his memory. He found his friend Recardo beside him and tried to call his name, but pain was striking all parts of his body.

He tried to wake his friend up several times without any reaction.

He tried to lift his legs to see whether they are fine, but he couldn't stand on them because of new earth gravity and wounds in his legs. He crawled to the treatment room to bandage some head injuries, bone breaking, and neck pains because of the spacecraft colliding. He crawled again towards his friend and tried to wake him up. He found a branch instilled in his body. He inspected his heart beats to find that he has already died. He was so sad. Andre took the feeding and analgesic pills with some water and lied in bed in order to heal. Three days have passed, and he gradually began to cure, however he couldn't walk without the stick and leaning on ship walls. After he got well he decided to bury his friend Recardo. He dragged him outside and dug a hole and buried him, putting some flowers on his tomb.

Not knowing whether life actually existed on such earth, he decided to search in the entire region by heading to the west from the early morning till sunset then return to the ship, and heading next day to the east till sunset. When he went southwards he found a pyramid-shaped mountain with snow on the top. It looked splendid. There was a small cave down the mountain, so he decided to stay in the cave as a warm and suitable place.

After four days of sweeping the region, he found no evidence of human life existence. He only found animals. He was preparing the small satellite to send signals to the earth notifying them about life on new-earth. The satellite was bounded to a rocket above the spacecraft. It takes just a hit of a button to open the upper doors to launch the rocket. But, there was a problem. Electric circuits didn't work, and there is no electricity. He had to connect it to work by computer and ship control room.

He had a comprehensive manual on the spacecraft and troubleshooting book; however, it was complicated and needed much time to read. He started to read the manual everyday in the light of a small lantern.

The next day, he was feeling hungry, eager to try normal food, Bored of the feeding pills and feeling weak, he decided to change his diet. He opened his cabinet and took his gun loading it with around 10 shots and took 10 more in case needed for reserve out of the 300 shots he had. He has never shot before and was very afraid to use the gun.

He went out hunting to finally find a rabbit which he could shot after a long chasing. It was his first time for hunting any animal and he was happy for that. Unfortunately, he lost his way back to the ship. He strived to find it till sunset. He sat by a tree tired and afraid, thinking what he might do if he lost his ship and disappointed the nations' hopes to save the world.

He sat down folding is arms and leaning his head on them, thinking what he might do. He decided to get some sleep to start searching again in the morning.

During midnight, he heard a sound of a woman screaming coming from far away. He got up looking all directions trying to find out whether it was a dream or real. It was really a sound of a woman, but not so clear.

He followed the sound and began to hear a voice of a child screaming. He ran quickly while the sounds became nearer, and he continued to run his way through the trees in the dark.

Coming nearer, a light appeared. He found three men, a women, a child around a fire and a man lying on the ground after being killed.

He was watching them, and saw a man saying: "quickly before anyone sees us". One of them was holding the woman's shoulders and closing her mouth, while the other was rapping her, and telling her:" shut up or we will kill your son." They were all laughing. Andre was watching them and wondering what he shall do.

He was hesitated to get out his gun to kill them fearing that they would kill him and vanish all efforts and hopes. He sympathized with the woman and couldn't decide whether or not he shall save her. He crawled till he came nearer and hid behind the tree.

- "we have to kill that child, or he will expose everything." The rapping man said.

- "come on child, come I will relief you from such cold and hunger forever." Said the man after getting up singing. He got out a knife to kill the child. At this moment Andre couldn't hold more and shoot him. He shot him under his stomach to fall immediately while the other two men ran away leaving the women. The man wore his pants and they all hid behind a rock screaming at their fellow lying on the ground.

They got out their swords and went to see their fellow. They were looking everywhere wondering about such strong sound that killed their fellow. He shot again but he missed them. Then he shot the second man in his chest to die immediately.

-"who are you?" the third man screamed, "please let me go." Andre was afraid and shivering which made it difficult to shot, especially while both women and child were screaming. The man tried to escape but Andre shot him once. He tried to crawl till finally Andre shot him dead.

Andre was walking slowly. The woman was crying and shivering and the child was crying too. She puts her hands on her head. He approached her not believing she war real.

-"are you ok?" said Andre

She looked at him and held her child between her arms. Went to the murdered man and held him while they were crying. She was tapping her husband's chest begging him to wake up, but in vain. Andre tried to draw the woman away from the murdered man, but she pushed him without uttering a single word.

He sat by the fire wondering what could he do. He didn't have any options but wait for the woman and the child. After two hours, the women stopped crying and felt asleep over the man's chest. He sat watching her wondering about such love that made the woman sleep on a dead man chest.

He decided to sleep as well. He woke up in the morning at the child's cries. The mother was still laying her head on her husband's chest with her tears on her cheeks. He was afraid to get near her again after pushing him the day before. She got up and nursed her child. She asked her if she was hungry. She looked up with her red eyes full of tears without talking. She looked at her child touching his cheeks gently.

He sat down thinking. Then he dragged the two criminal's away next do the third one who was trying to escape. He took some woods and started a fire and began to roast the rabbit. He cut the rabbit into two halves and gives it to the woman and returned again next to the fire. He sat down eating, while the woman sat without making any move and without looking at him. He didn't know what language she speaks. The night came while she was still sitting turning her eyes between the dead man and the child.

He fell asleep to wake up again to find the child playing and the food still not eaten. He looked for the woman where he found her digging a hole in the ground.

He was hesitated to help her fearing she would hit him with the sword in her hands. He watched her till she finished and threw the sword on the floor. She wanted to drag the dead man to but he was big and heavy. She looked at him. He understood what she wanted and they dragged him to the hole. They put the man in the hole and she sat on the dust filling back the hole and crying. She held the tomb. He sat pitifully watching the woman and wondering what had happened to them.

The woman remained as she was till her child cried, while he was still watching them. She took the sword in a hand and her child in another hand and handed him the sword saying: "my husband doesn't need the sword now, it's yours, thank you."

It was the best words he needed to hear at this time. He nodded smiling to her and she went to feed her child. The night came while they were sitting by the fire and the woman was breastfeeding her child to help him get sleep. She put the child down and asked him about his name.

-" Andre, and yours?"

- "Jessey."

-"I want to ask you, how did you kill them alone while you don't seem a warrior. I don't even see a sword with you.

-"I used this."

-"does this kill?" asked Jessey wondering. And she approached to see how it worked.

-"you just push that button and the shot will come out to kill others."

- "Aha."

- "Hold it."

She tried to hold it but she put it back.

-"I have a question for you, what is your story? And why are you here alone? And do other people live here?"

-"it's a long story. My husband was a strong warrior. No one ever defeated him. The king used to celebrate his thrown anniversary every year by choosing the strongest warriors to fight each other while he watches. Some died, others get injured or disabled." Jessey continues her story: "King Walter used to bet on my husband who always won. One day I dreamt that my husband fell in a hole. I got up scarred and asked him not to go to the anniversary. He told me he needed money and the winner will receive 100 gold pieces from the king. My husband needed money for our living. My husband Aleksandro was chosen to fight against a warrior called The Ghost, as they called him because he was fast. The fight began between my husband and the other warrior. The fight was fierce and my husband knocked the Ghost down. We were clapping for him and he waved his hand for the audience who were calling his name Aleksandro, Aleksandro, kill him, kill him. The Ghost was lying on the floor

trying to get up and took a knife while looking at me. I screamed.
Hardly had my husband looked back than he hit his right leg right
behind his knee with the knife. My husband screamed and was about
to fall, then cut off the Ghost's head. I was putting my hand on my
mouth. I felt as if it's me who was hit with the knife. I was pregnant
and I felt I was about to lose my child out of fear. The audience
clapped to him while he took the knife out of his leg. He got out of
the court and I rushed to him.

"Aleksandro, my love, did you get seriously hurt?"

"Don't worry my dear."

But he couldn't walk. He was pulling his right leg. I held his hand
till we reached home. He laid in bed and I inspected his injury to
find it was really deep. I rushed to the doctor and asked him to come.
He was very busy, as the ceremony included twenty fights resulted in
dead and injured. I begged him to come promising to pay him what
he want till he agreed. He was walking slowly and I begged him to
hurry to the house. The doctor inspected my husband who was
moaning with pain. The doctor said his injury was severe and the
nerves were cut. He said he might not be able to walk except if
nerves grew again. I begged them to treat him. He bandaged the
injury and I helped him. My husband was biting my clothes out of
pain and holding my hand strongly. He said he would see him the
next day. The next day my husband was really tired the doctor gave
him some herbs. Two months later he couldn't walk on his leg. He
refused to lean on me as I was pregnant, and insisted on trying on
his own. Four months later I delivered my baby Sofia. By that time
he was lame and could only stand up using a stick. Unfortunately, a
message came to from the king that they released him from the army
and we have to leave or pay the taxes. Those who can't pay the
monthly taxes are sent to the hill's valley to live without food or
protection and his children would live as slaves. Taxes are levied on
everyone except the army. I agreed to work to be able to pay the
monthly taxes. I searched for a job till I worked for a family with my
daughter, but they found her noisy and were bored with her screams.
They told me either to come alone without my daughter or leave
work.

- *"and why don't you leave her with your husband?"*

- *"I couldn't leave her without breastfeeding. I searched for another job and found a kind lady whom I served her family only for little wage to pay the taxes. They were paying me on time as they know our case. One day it was only me with my daughter Sophia and Admero.*

- *"who is Admero?"*

- *"the house owner who used to pay me. He worked for the army. I was cleaning the rug. He called me and when I went to him put his hands on my back and held me strongly. He was trying to kiss me, while I was screaming ordering him to stop. He slapped me on my face and knocked me down.*

> *"Do you want to live with your husband and daughter?"*

> *"Yes, but not that way."*

> *"Listen." He approached," I will pay you more.*

> *"No."*

He pulled my hair to outside the house and told me not to come back. I spitted on him and left holding my daughter who woke up at the screams. I went home trying to hide my tears. He was wondering my early return. I couldn't by then hold my tears. I held him and cried hard.

> *"What's up. Tell me."*

- *" I couldn't tell him. I only told him that they fired me again. He held me in his arms and told me that son he will be fine and search for a job. We couldn't take it anymore. Whenever officers come to collect the taxes I beg them to wait for another week. Till the day came the guards came ordering us to leave the Empire. My husband was screaming:*

> *"How could you get me out of the Empire?! Don't you know me? I'm Aleksandro, no one has ever defeated me."*

I was trying to calm him down while he was trying to attack them. I feared they might kill him.

"Yes we do know you. You used to be a strong man before, but now you became the weakest man as if you became an elderly." They said laughing sarcastically. "Hurry up, you have to leave within one day. If you don't leave without you heads you and you wife and daughter."

-*"I tried to relief him and said I would live with him forever even in a forest full of wolves. I held him in my arms while he was crying like a child. At the morning we collected our things to leave to the Hill's Valley. I have never seen the village, but only heard that no taxes are levied there, and it is inhibited with old, disabled, or insane. It s a deprived village.*

-*"and who guards it?" asked Andre.*

-*"No one." She said. "If you can protect yourself, otherwise you will get killed. I walked with my husband very slowly till we reached the middle of the road. We reached such miserable place at sunset. My husband decided to rest till morning. I gathered some wood while he was caring for my daughter. He started a fire and we sat eating some bread till suddenly three men attacked us with swords and knifes. All I can remember that he was holding two of them trying to knock them down but he was sitting. The third one was trying to hit him from the back with a knife. He was screaming telling me to escape but I couldn't leave him alone. Either we live together or die together. I tried to push the third one who was trying to hit him."* Jessey stopped talking and began to cry. *"He pushed me and they killed my husband. I screamed loudly and called for help. Then, all happened as you saw. You know the rest. He lived as a hero and died as a hero."*

-*"What a story!" said Andre, "and what would you do now?"*

-*"I really don't know. We have no choice but go to the Hill's Valley. It will take about one day walking from here. What about your story? How did you know about our place? And why are you here?"*

-*"My story is very long not as short as yours. If I told you my story may be I won't finish it in a day, or a month, or a year, or even more."*

-*"really?"*

-" yes, and if you wonder how I knew about you place, GOD sent me to you."

-"How?"

-" I decided to hunt a rabbit, I was chasing him and it was very fast. After I hunted him I lost my way and didn't know how to return to my place. I was lost between the trees trying to find my way back. It was then sunset so I decided to sleep till morning to find my way again. While I was deeply sleeping I woke up at screaming. I looked in all directions to follow the sound and I ran towards the sound till it disappeared to hear the voice of the child crying. I followed the voice till I came here.

-"does anyone live with you?"

-"No, I live alone."

She held his hand and thanked him for saving their lives.

-"I owe you a favor. I don't know about your story, I only know that you saved me and my daughter."

Jessey left and went to sleep by her daughter to be ready for the next day journey.

Day of departure

-"take the clothes of one of those criminals to wear it, you clothes will make you suspicious." Jessey said.

He took off the clothes of one of them to wear it.

On their way, he asked her: "How did you know your husband, and how did you fell in love with him? Pardon me if this question bothers you, or revives your memories. I only want to know the secret about such love. I have never been in love before.

-"really? I thought you are married."

-"no, I have never been in love. I haven't met any girl since I was eleven.

Jessey started to tell him the love story - One day my father was going out.

-"I am going to the king anniversary ceremony." My father told my mother.

-"I want to go with you, daddy." I said.

-"No, your mother needs your help."

-"My mother worked as a tailor she rent dresses, and I help her with the delivery."

-"Please take me with you, daddy. Mum, may I go with daddy?"

-"I don't think so. You will not stand scenes there, blood and disgusting scenes, murder and cutting.

-"Don't worry, mum. I am not afraid."

-"Ok, take care."

-"let's go then." My father said.

It was a great day and large audience went to see the king's anniversary. I was 16 and my mother did not want me to see blood scenes. She didn't like it and have never been there except once. I was watching the fights when I first saw Aleksandro. He was handsome strong man with long and smooth hair. He was fighting and I was cheering, I was standing. sitting and watching , I was very excited. I used to stand and clap when he won. I was smiling and calling his name with the audience Aleksandro, Aleksandro. When the fight was over, I went to see him, I really liked him. He was going out of the court. He saw me and smiled to me. I was shy and he was looking at me and smiling. I ran towards my father happily.

"You are happy today." Said my father.

"Yes daddy." I said while hugging him.

"A year later, I attended the ceremony again with my father, and I went to see him again after the fight. He was walking with another person, I greeting him saying:

"Hi"

"Hi, sweetie."

I was sweating and I ran away. I felt him watching me. When I sat in my place I looked to see him standing with the person and pointing towards me. I sat next to my father. I was the happiest girl in the world. When I went back home I laid in bed imagining him. I imagined my hero. A year later, my father was very sick and he was in a coma he couldn't feel anything. I decided to go alone. I wore my best clothes and went to see my hero hitting strongly with his sword. I went after the fight to greet him as usual. I passed by him and couldn't stare at him, I was shy.

"Hi, prince of Empire."

"Hi, princess of Empire."

I laughed and went on my way. He followed me and held my hands asking:

"What is your name?"

"Jessey."

"And, my name is Aleksandro."

"You are known to everyone." I said laughing.

"Where do you live."

"I live in that place."

"Can I see you tonight?" he asked.

I was embarrassed. I nodded twice "yes". I went home in great joy. I kissed my parents.

"I can see you happy today" said my mother.

I went to bed breathing rapidly. My heart was beating violently. I was looking at the ceiling imagining him. At sunset I went out.

"Where are you going?" my mother asked.

"I will come back soon."

"Ok, don't be late." My mother said.

I waited for him till I despaired. I was waiting for three years for this love I wanted him to be my hero.

I was looking in all directions. I was moving so he can see me, but he didn't come. I went home thinking I am dump to expect a person like Aleksandro to fall in love with me. I went home sad and disappointed. I thought he was thinking of another woman and many other thoughts. I went home and knocked the door.

"Who is it." My mother asked.

"Jessey."

"What's up, are you ok? You seem pale."

"Yes, mum I'm fine."

"Ok, clean the house and go to bed."

While I was cleaning the door knocked, I thought one of the neighbors asking about my father as they all loved him. I opened the door to find Aleksandro.

"Aleksandro!!" I screamed.

"Who's at the door?" my mother asked.

"No one, no one." I replied her.

He whispered: "Hi, I'm really sorry. It's late now. I was invited for a dinner with the king. I couldn't escape it. We will meet tomorrow in the same place."

"Ok." I replied smiling.

"Good bye."

I closed the door.

"Who's at the door?" my mother asked.

"No one, I was going out for some breeze."

"Come on. Let's sleep now, we have a lot of work tomorrow."

I went to bed thinking was very cruel to judge him. I couldn't sleep. I was imagining him. His image was always in front of me. When I woke up in the morning I saw the sun with its splendid shine and orange color. I got up and went to my mother to find her sewing the clothes.

"Good morning, mum."

"Good morning my dear."

I went to dad and kissed him. I was waiting sunset. My mother was at dad's room. I got out at sunset, and it was only few minutes when he appeared.

"Hi." Greeted Aleksandro.

"Hi." I replied.

"'I'm really sorry about yesterday." Aleksandro said.

"Never mind. I forgot about it. What's up."

"Can you believe I was looking for you for a year, when I was with my friend last year and you told me hi, I told you hi sweetie. You ran away, and my friend asked me who were you. I told him I saw you here last year.

"Do you know her name?" My friend asked.

"No." I replied.

"Go then and know her name"

I followed you but the court was full of people, I couldn't find you. And since then I have been thinking about you. Whenever I see any girl in town I thought that she was you. I was praying to GOD to find you again."

-"Actually, I was not intending to come. My father is very sick. But I didn't want to miss your fight, I used to watch you every year." I said.

"You know what I liked about you?"

"What?"

"Your magic eyes and your smile, I couldn't forget it since we first met."

"I couldn't stand his words and looked down feeling extremely shy. I couldn't look at his eyes while he was saying such words."

"Don't hide your beautiful eyes." He held my head and raised it up.

"Stop that." I said laughing.

"Look at my eyes."

Couldn't do that. I was very shy.

"I can't be late today. I didn't tell my mother I was going out.:

"Well, we will meet tomorrow." He said.

I hurried and when I reached home he was still standing. I waved to him good bye. A week passed and he was always telling me his war stories and how brave he was. A week later, my father died. It was the worst day in my life. My mother fell sick after my father died. He used to pass daily by our house asking about my mother and asking whether I needed any help. He never stopped asking about me. He used to give me money. I always refuse to take it, so he would leave it on the table and go away. I sat with my mother for three months. I didn't meet him by that time as she was really sick due to her sorrow for my father. My suffering increased as my mother's sickness worsened. I expected him to be bored and leave me. One day, he knocked the door and asked to talk with me. I thought he would leave me. We sat by the house wall to hear my mother's call.

"It is time now, I want to marry you. I love you. I know it's not the right time as your father has just died. I will compensate your father's love. What do you say?"

I couldn't say anything, just a tear appeared telling everything. He kissed me and held me in his warm arms.

"You are the best."

My mother called me. I stood up and whipped my tears.

"Do you think it is appropriate no to tell you mother after the death of your father?"

"Yes, she is better now."

"Well then, I will come tomorrow."

He came and met my mother and told her he was asking me to marry him.

> *"Thanks God, I found someone to care for my daughter after my death. May God bless your marriage."*

We held the marriage gathering.

I was very happy. He was a father before being a husband. I used to call him sometimes father.

She began to cry.

-"Are you fine?" Asked Andre.

-"Yes. I used to call him "my pony" as he had thick long and smooth hair like the horse. I liked to play with his hair. He didn't like such name, but I liked it. He was saying if I'm your pony, you are my horseman. Four months later, my mother died. I sorrowed her death. He was sympathizing with me. He told me I have more responsibilities now. I was a father, now a father and mother. I cried many times in his arms. And then all things happened as you know.

-"What a story! I'm really sorry for what happened to you."

-"Thank you." Said Jessey. "What will you do now?"

- "I don't know. But I will accompany you to a safe place at the village and make sure you are fine. May be I can find someone to guide me through my way."

The first visit to the Hill's Village

They reached the village he heard about. He saw the patient, the disabled, the injured, and the insane. However, they were all smiling and greeting their guests.

The village was highly populated and inhabitants were sharing food and water together. They were like brothers.

A day later, Andre searched for someone to guide him to a pyramid-shaped mountain with a cave.

Suddenly, Empire guards came to the village looking for servants and slaves for the king. The guard leader walked through the peoples looking arrogantly at them, and people looking back at him in hatred. He saw Aleksandro's wife and knew her, as she was known for her beauty and beautiful eyes.

The guard stopped his horse: "Oh, Great warrior Aleksandro's wife." he said greeting her.

-"Hi!".Replied Jessey.

-"Where is your disabled husband?" Asked the guard.

Jessey remained silent.

-"Do you hear me? Where is you disabled husband?"

- "My husband has died."

- "Mum, and how did he die?"

-"Murderers attacked us and killed him."

-"And how did you and your daughter survived?"

- "We ran away till we came here."

-"and where did your husband die?"

-"I don't know."

-"You are mine, then."

He walked down the horse and grasped her hair. "Dou you know, I used to envy your husband for two things, his strength and his wife."

-"We only found two girls, sir."

-"And the third is mine." Said the guard leader.

- "No, please. I have a child. Please let me go for the sake of your friend Aleksandro. He was you fellow." Screamed Jessey.

-"Take her." Ordered the Leader.

-"I think we can have a look to find any girl hiding before we go." Suggested a guard.

Andre was asking about the pyramid mountain when he suddenly saw a crown around a child girl crying.

-"It's Sophia." Said Andre.

-"The guards came and took her, her mother told us give her to Andre."

-"Where did they go?"

-"We heard them saying that they would take a tour in the village."

-"Which way did they go?"

-"This way."

He rushed towards their direction and hid waiting for them. He checked his gun and found three shots while they were four *guards. He wondered what he can do. He decided to take the risk and use the sword if necessary.*

-"Sir, what will you do with the woman, will you give her to the king?"Asked the guard.

- "No, it's mine. I'll rape her." replied the Leader.

-"She is beautiful, let's give her to the king and have our reward.:

-"Shut up, she is mine, not for the king. I give the king everything. I just want her to be mine."

-"Stop.!" Andre appeared on their way.

The horses stopped.

-"Don't move. Leave Jessey and anyone with her."

-"So, who's it beauty?"

-"He is the one who saved my life, and he will save me now."

-"Is it the new lover?" said the leader laughing. "And what is it in your hand?" asked carelessly.

-"Leave the girl and I'll let you survive." Ordered Andre.

-"What if we didn't leave her?"

-"You can try!"

-"What have you just said?" the Leader asked walking down the horse.

-"I said leave the girl or I'll smash you head."

-"Then you'll be buried together." Hardly did the Leader raise his sword screaming than a bullet penetrated his chest and he felt down."

Two guards walked down and the third was holding Jessey. They tried to attack him, so he shot them all dead. He had no bullets remaining.

-" You want to die?" asked Andre approaching the guard.

-"No." He nodded his head.

- "Fine, then. Let her go and you go to your children and family. Tell you king that you were released to deliver a message."

-"What message?"

- "Tell him that the village now has a ruler protecting it."

The guards released Jessey and those who were with her and returned back to the Empire.

-"Thank you again. I owe you my life." She said hugging him. "You saved me, and I 'all do anything for you." She kissed him for the first time.

They returned to the Hill's valley with things they collected. People crowded around them and asked them how they survived. A girl told the people the story.

-"You'll make us all die." A man said. "Let's celebrate our last day, folks."

-"I'm sorry, I didn't mean to cause you any harm. I only wanted to take back what they took from me. I'll go."

- "Where will you go, son. They will come to the village and kill us. You will not be able to go far away and they will find you." Said elderly Yemen.

-"We will fight them. We will not make it easy." Said Andre.

-"How will we do that with a missing arm?" said a man.

-"Or with a missing leg!" said another man.

-"Or with missing limbs" said another crawling.

- "How long does it take them to come here?" asked Andre.

-"It takes 3 or 4 days for a large army to come here." Said Yemen."Or one day and a half for a small division."

- "And how large is his army?" asked Andre.

-" 60,000 soldiers or even more."

-"And much do you expect him to send?"

-"10,000 if he has mercy for us."

- "Listen, can anyone guide me to a large pyramid with a cave?"

-"Yes, I know that mountain. It is in the south. I used to go there for worship when I was young." replied an old man.

-"Please tell me where it is." Begged Andre.

-"Wait till sunset."

When it was sunset, the old man guided Andre to the mountain:

-"Do you see that star? The triangle?" said the old man.

-" Yes."

-"Go towards that star, you'll just hit the mountain."

-"How long does it take?" asked Andre.

-" Four days walk, and one day and a half ride, one day if the horse is fast and healthy."

He went to Jessey.

-"Let's run away now and live in the mountain. We'll die here."

- "What about the people here? You and I'll cause their death."
said Jessey.

- "What can we do?! Just look at them, they are not even able
to fight. We'll just die."

-"You saved my life, and you can save theirs also. I also have
an avenge for blood. Don't you remember what they did to me
and my husband? I can't live with you if you're coward and
fear death. I wish now you haven't saved me to be with my
brave husband. My husband lived as a brave man and dies as a
brave man. If I have to run away I'll run away with my
daughter but I won't live with you. " Said Jessey.

-"I can't fight. I fear I would die. I'm not here for war, I came
here for a certain task."

-"Do you remember when you told me that Allah sent you to
save you. You are here to save them from misery and unjust.

-"God sent me to save you, but look at them. They can't even
hold a sword. How do you want me to fight against thousands
alone." said Andre.

-"I'll be with you, and they all will support you. They all need a
strong leader like you."

He left angrily and rode his horse. He returned and stopped
before the tent to see if she would change her mind. She went
out of the tent with her daughter.

-"Stay. Stay for my sake and for the sake of my daughter, stay
for the sake of you people." said Jessey looking up to him.

-"No way!" Andre nodded his head.

He left on his horse to be shortly stopped by Yemen.

-"I have always believed that one day God will send us someone who will save us. I pray to God not to disappoint us again. You have our souls in your hand now, either you save our lives, or you leave and come back after a while to see us hanged. May God bless your path.

-"These people must be insane. Did they find anyone else to save them? How can I fight a whole army with a gun containing 280 shots?" thought Andre on his way on the horse.

It was like a miracle. He reached the place before sunset and followed his way to his ship. He was tired and lay on his bed trying to sleep. He couldn't sleep. He was thinking of Jessey and other people. He was trying to find a solution. But the equation was 30,000+ 280 shots= death. It's impossible to save their lives.

-"I'm sorry Jessey, I can't." cried Andre.

He continued crying till he fell asleep. In his dreams he heard the steps of the army from the mountain. He ran towards the Hill's valley to see the village burnt. Dead bodies were everywhere. He searched for Jessey to find her hanged on a cross with nuts.

-"Jessey! Are you ok?"

-"You are late. Take care of my daughter. Take care of yourself." Replied Jessey slowly.

Suddenly a man came talking from behind him.

-"So, the new lover is here." The soldier said digging the knife in Andre's heart.

He woke up.

He was reminding himself that he was here for a task, not for love or war. He took the ship manuals to learn how to regain power and electricity for the ship and how to fire the rocket. He found a page giving instructions on how to fire an anti-body rocket to the space. He was astonished and tried to find its location.

He found a page about how to repair the rocket and saw in the book two rockets.

-"That's it." He said hitting the book with his hand. "30,000+two rockets= victory."

Now the equation is fair. He found the two rockets under the airplane and began to read about using the rocket. He found wires connected to the rocket. He read more about how to repair the rocket and found that the battery helps the rocket to be fired. He cut off the wires and took the two rockets which were really heavy. He wasn't sure if the horse could hold them, and any mistake or fall will ruin everything.

He followed the instructions to install the batteries and found it at the airplane tail. He found two batteries, but he couldn't get it out. He quickly got a screw driver and got them out and took it.

The problem now that he will not be able to ride the horse if he put the rockets and batteries on it. Also the horse will be slower and he will have to walk which will delay him three days.

He sat down thinking. He thought about making a carriage, but it will take him a week to make it. He searched in his ship for a solution. He found two wheel chairs made of iron. But wheels may get broken. But there was no other option. He wrapped both rockets in two blankets and tied them with ropes to protect them from falling. He put the two chairs opposite to each other and put the rockets on them. He thought about welding the chairs but no electricity is available in the ship. He put the rockets and fastened them tightly.

Now he had to think how he would fix them behind the horses to make them stable. He went to search for some wood and returned back to fix the wood on the arm chair and fix it tightly from both right and left sides and connect it to the horse then tie it.

He took 280 shots and some food pills and medicines with analgesic and needles and left making the star behind him and headed towards the village.

Empire

The guard entered the empire's gate quickly, and got off his horse's back. He ran towards the palace and said, "I want to meet the king right now".

He entered the palace, where there were 4 senate's members .

The guard was very tired. He was breathing deeply when he said, "Your Majesty, Commander and two soldiers were killed in hill's village   ."

The King stood up .

"Who killed them? How they were killed?" The King asked .

"Some person obstructed our way. He was handling something, which was looking like a rod of iron or a magic stick, something that I do not know, sounds terrible and kills people. Commander and two guards were killed and the person kept me alive to deliver you a message: the village now has a master and a leader to protect" The guard said .

"How does he look like? Does he look like a worrier? Is he a huge bodied? Is he a human being like us?" The king asked .

"No your majesty" Guard said, "He does not look like a worrier. He looks a normal person".

"Ok, you may leave" the King said .

"Here comes the person who shall get rid of us, the empire and the Gods. All happened because of you" Eric said, then went out to call the rest of the senate's members for an emergency meeting .

News spread all over the city that a strong man with magic powers became the leader of Hill's village. Blacksmith, heard about the news. He quickly prepared his horse, he filled his cart with iron tools, swords and armors. And covered the cart with counterpane, then he moved towards the hill in order to avenge his daughter.

46

The Meeting

The council met with the king to discuss what happened.

They were very anxious.

-"My Lord, release the priestess out of jail, she is the only one who can help us and save us." Said Eric.

-"Shut up, has the priestess ever saved our city? And how do you think a single person can fight against a whole army.

-"But we heard he has a magic stick." Said the council head.

-"Nonsense, nothing called a magic stick exists. If there was really a magic stick, that insane which would have made it? It is my war, and you'll see how I'll hang him at the city gate. Tomorrow the army will move. Even if he has a magic stick, he will not be able to defeat my army. He will not stand for long. I'll get rid of him.

The king ended the meeting.

-"I just don't like such war, if the king just agreed to the priestess, all this wouldn't have happened." Said Babel the council head. "I can only say that God will not disappoint us. Let's pray for God's help."

They all left. And at the morning bells rang and the horn was whistled. People and army gathered.

-"For hundreds of years you have been living in prosper of antecessors. You have been eating, drinking, entertaining in peace, and it's time now to pay back the favor. There is a person claiming another God and another king, he want to ruin you and your empire. He has a magic stick that kills people. Don't believe anything unless you see it. He is a wicked

priestess. And now we are ready to destroy him. Prepare your luggage, swords, and armors. Farewell you loved ones, and at sunset we will leave. And I'll be the first.

-"Long live the king. Long live God. Long live the king, long live God." Replied his people.

At the morning, thousands of armies began to move, while Andre was also moving towards Hill village.

Andre reached Hill village.

The village was saying that the king arrived. Jessey heard the voices and got out quickly and hugged him.

-"I knew you would come back. I have been praying for you." Jessey said.

-"I know that God has sent me to save you and save the miserable."

-"Someone wants to talk to you." Said Yemen.

-"I'm the blacksmith. I heard about the news and escaped the Empire to help you." said blacksmith who told Andre the story of his daughter and what the king did to him. "I'm at your service. I'm ready to do anything you order. I've swords and iron armors."

-"Give weapons to anyone who can fight, and repair the gate to make it unbreakable."

-"Yes, sir." answered blacksmith.

At the morning, crowds gathered and he went up stage.

-*"People, you know that Walter's army is coming. I was the one who caused such war, and I will finish it. I am here to protect you. I want to know who desires to join the army in war."*

-*"All of us. All of us."*

-*"We were waiting for a person like you to lead us. We are fed up of humiliation and slavery. We are at your request, Lord."* Yemen said, then bowed and they all bowed.

Jessey was watching him with her daughter and smiling and she bowed as well.

-*"Listen, don't attack. I only want you to defend the village and the gate. I don't want them to get through the gate. Anyone who can fight go to blacksmith to receive what he wants."*

-*"Long live the king. Long live the king."*

The people went to blacksmith and got swords and armors.

The first order was to make a military base at the gate and a control tower and allow no one to enter or exit without his permission. He took the rockets to the tent. It was wrapped in blankets. He put them on his bed and sat down reading the instruction manual, till Jessey entered.

-*"Any orders from my lord? Is he hungry?"*

-*"Come and sit her. I hope you won't call me Lord again."* He said laughing.

She sat beside him.

-*"Where is your daughter?"*

-*"She is sleeping in the tent. What is it that thing?"*

49

-"This is what I was searching for, it's a valuable treasure. It'll give us victory."

-"Did you come back for me?" she asked looking in his eyes.

-"And for whom else will I come back!"

She kissed him. They kissed and laid together in bed. Jessey got out of bed and kissed his head and left to sleep with her daughter. He held her hand.

-"You don't have to sleep in the other tent. Come and bring you daughter and sleep here."

-"Ok."

At the morning, he saw guards standing at his tent and was astonished to see their organization.

-"How did you learn all this?" asked Andre.

-"We were soldiers serving the Emperor, some got injured or disabled and couldn't pay the taxes so we came here."

-"Well, call blacksmith and tell him to come to the tent."

-"Yes, sir."

Blacksmith rushed to the tent.

-"Yes, sir."

-"Loose the tie from the rocket. I want a long pipe to fix that thing on it so that it doesn't move forward or backward, and to direct it to any location as I wish."

-"What is it, sir?"

-"You'll know later."

-"I'm sorry, sir. Can I take this thing with me?"

-"No."

-"Ok, I'll measure the length and width. I'll bring a rope to take the measurements."

Andre made a mock firing. He put the rocket on his shoulder and thought of how it will be directed. They began to search for a solution. Blacksmith was offering some advice about how to fix the rocket. He thought about making a front cap for the pipe, so that it falls down when the rocket is fired.

-"Hurry up, we have no time." Andre ordered.

-"ok, I'll begin to work right away." Said blacksmith.

One day later, the Emperor army was approaching, while people were still working hard at the Hill village. As the army approached, Andre got more worried. What if it didn't work and he died. He was very irritated.

-"They have reached, sir." Said a guard rushing to him.

He ran towards the control tower and saw a huge army approaching nearer and nearer.

-"Call blacksmith."

Blacksmith rushed to him.

-"Yes, sir."

-"Have you finished?"

-"Yes, sir, and it's ready. Where do you want it?"

-"I want it here at the control tower."

The control tower was a long passage above the gate.

He ordered his soldiers to carry the rockets and put it up. They were ready to receive the orders. The army was approaching and they were watching.

War

The king came to the front.

-"I'm King Walter of the great Empire. I order you to surrender. Surrender is bravery. And you wicked magician. Get out and show us yourself. Don't cause innocents and elderly and children to die. I warn you. I" destroy the whole village. No one will survive. I'll kill also children rather than adults. If you surrender I'll forgive you. I only want the magician and don't defend him. I'll give you one and a half day. If you don't open the gate I'll destroy the village."

The king returned back to the army.

Andre was watching everything and was worried.

Everything was ready. The rocket is in place and all locations are protected. He took the battery and put it under the rocket. But the wire was short. He called blacksmith again and ordered him to bring two iron skewers.

-"I don't have any iron, sir, nor fire. I have an idea. I have two swords. Will it work?"

-"Yes, bring them. Make holes in the upper part of the swords. I want to insert this wire like a needle and a thread."

Blacksmith quickly made the holes in the upper part of the swords.

He called two soldiers and explained how to connect the swords to the battery.

-"Put the swords when I tell you. You stand here and you stand here."

-"Yes, sir."

Time was running. The king came.

-"Your grace period is over. You are now my enemies. I wish I get off you head, And I'll hang you till you get rotten."

The king returned again with armors and ordered the army to get ready.

The sound of the army was frightening.

-"Come on. Take you positions. Throw your arrows."

The soldiers rushed to protect Andre from the arrows.

-"Attack them." ordered the king.

The soldiers began to attack.

He prepared his gun and ordered the soldiers to get ready.

-"They are coming. Connect the swords when I tell you."

-"Yes, sir."

He waited till they approached.

He carried the rocket on his shoulder to direct it but the arrows were so many. They approached even more.

-"Get ready, 1, 2, 3 com on connect." Andre ordered.

The rocket was fired towards them and exploded throwing dead bodies everywhere, even some were thrown into the village and some were burnt. A huge ole was made in the ground and the army retreated.

-"don't get back come on, attack them." The king screamed.

The second line moved forward.

Andre was fixing the second rocket and fired it when the second line of soldiers approached. An arrow got him in his shoulder and knocked him down. Soldiers rushed to him.

-"Don't worry. Take you places. Come on 1, 2, 3." he said after he stood up again.

He fired the second rocket which was stronger than the first. Dead bodies scattered, and some soldiers escaped while others retreated. He took off his gun shooting one after another.

No soldiers were remaining. And the king ordered the army to retreat: "Get back, get back."

The king retreated and went back to the empire.

-"We beat. We beat." People said.

They hugged each other and celebrated the great victory for the first time in its history. Andre fell down and they carried him to the room.

A person called Arthur came. He was not really a physician, but he knows how to deal with wounds and he treats some injured.

Arthur came and so did Jessey.

She hugged him while she was crying.

-"Are these tears of joy or sadness?"

-"For you and for the victory."

She helped him getting off the arrow in his left shoulder. They got out the arrow and the injury was a minor.

Jessey spent all night caring for him.

At the morning, Jessey was sleeping after caring for him all night.

-" Where is the gun?" he asked frightened.

-"What is a gun? Do you mean this?"

-"Yes. I was afraid that someone will grab it. Put it under my pillow and give me some food pills.

She brought all the pills.

-"That's it." He said taking the analgesic.

-"What is this?"

- "Analgesic, it makes me not feel the pain."

-"How do you make it?"

-"It's a long story. I'll tell you later."

King lost the war

It was a painful loss to the king, He returned angry and entered the city. The voices of shrieking women can be heard in all the empire, women became widows, children became orphans, people are either a mother bereaved of her son or a child bereaved of his father.

The king entered the palace and sat on his throne and asked the minister how much soldiers remain.

The minister replied: Sir, only twenty five thousand soldiers.

King said: prepare them to the war and I want the priestess here.

The soldiers went to bring her from prison chained with iron.

King asked her: Can you make a magic stick like the one with your friend the magician

She nodded her head: yes

He asked her how?: she said, angrily, your daughter and spat on the ground

The king gets so angry He said: Torture her until the last breath without food nor water

The Senate members came to know what happened in the battle, the king told them get out I don't want to see anyone.

Susan his wife entered

She said: My dear what's the matter with you, this is a war you lose today and tomorrow they will lose

King said: Yes, that is what I plan, I must find a way to kill that man.

Oh, if you see what kind of magic he has got, He explode fire on the ground, I almost died in this war

She said: Thank God for your safety, my darling Come with me,

I prepared warm water and wine for you to thing well.

The next day, the Senate members met the King.

The king stood and said: I lost yesterday in the war, but I will not lose this time.

The minister entered: your majesty there a disaster.

King said angrily: Can you see us in meeting

Minister: Sorry but it is so important

King: What is it

Minister: half of our army seceded and joined the Hill's valley army.

King: Dam it, when

Minister: this morning

King: how many

Minister: I do not know, nearly 8000 soldiers they are great fighters.

King: and how much we have left

Minister: Nearly 17000 soldiers, 5000 of the city guards & 12000 soldiers remained.

King: Oh damn it, prepare them for the war even the Guards.

Babel: Oh your majesty, nobody will stay here?, Admit it, soldiers lost in the battle.

King: Not a word, I'm the king here, and I destroy them till no soldier remain.

The King rise and said: The meeting has ended and He went out of the room

Senates: were angry and discuss how to fix that matter and they realized that they are dead

Eric said: I will save you all, I have a plan

Senates : How

Eric: will you see

Eric went in haste to the king and said: Your majesty, Let me lead in this war, I have a plan.

*The King laughed and said: Do you want to lead the war with
the priestess*

*Eric Said: No I will lead in the battlefield I have a plan that
nobody could think of.*

King said: What is your plan?

*Eric said: I'll take the soldiers and pretend that we want to join
them and get into them, the battle will then be in the village and
I will kill them all.*

King said: good idea and what if they discovered the matter

*Eric Said: How will they discover, they even don't know me, But
they know you well.*

*King sat down to think a little bit, then he said: if you win in this
battle, you will be the viceroy.*

Eric said: This is an honor for me your majesty.

King: Then take some soldiers with you.

*Eric said: No, sir, I want all the soldiers I will divide them into 2
some inside and others outside*

King said: No

Eric: As you wish your majesty.

*In the morning, King said to Eric: You will be the army
commander*

*The king declared that Eric is the army commander and
ordered to equip the soldiers.*

*Eric said: Get ready, He organized the army and 4000 troops
move towards the hill*

It was rainy

*When they were halfway to the village He raised his hand and
said stop here*

*Eric Got off his horse back and said: You know why the king
sent you*

They said for the war, sir.

Eric Said: Do you know what will happen to you there in the hill's village

They said: We know, sir,

Eric said: the King has sent you to die and you have seen what had happened to your colleagues two days ago, some of them have joined the other army, do you want to kill your friends?

Eric sat and looked at their faces and said, I can see that you are so afraid

Eric said: Do you want to die

They said: No, sir

Do you want to return to your families unharmed

They said yes, sir

He said: If so, I will be the new king, help me to get rid of the King who wants to destroy us and destroy the empire.

They raised up and shout: long live the King Eric, long live the King Eric

He said: I want some soldiers to go back with me now, and you stay here until I send you a note to go back to the empire.

He returned back quickly and with 300 soldiers.

He entered the palace and said your majesty

The king stands: Why have you returned?

Eric: Sir, there is a problem, A powerful torrent has closed the road to the Hill's Valley and three soldiers died while crossing the Torrent course, Do you want me to order the army to go forward or to return?

King said: Let them come back and go tomorrow

Eric told the guard: Let them return

Eric had a conversation with the King about how necessary is the plan success tomorrow after the rain.

Suddenly voices of the soldiers and the sound of swords

transcends.

King stood up shocked: What is happening

*Unexpectedly guards entered the room : Your majesty it is a
coup against you, then some guards got inside and killed them*

The King was so enraged: you dare to it Eric.

Eric: get down on your knees and I will forgive you

*King said: Kings don't kneel Have you forgot who am I - he
shouted and said, I am the King, He took out his sword*

Then the guards of Eric killed the King.

*Eric said: I was so merciful with you, I told you to kneel but you
didn't, You have demolished what our fathers and grandfathers
made in one day and I'm here to fix everything and soldiers
shouting long live King Eric long live King Eric*

Eric: Ask the Senate to come

*All of them came and He said: I have kept my promise and there
is something left to return the empire as powerful as it was
before.*

Do you accept me as your king.

They said unanimously: Yes

*They rang bells and trumpets were announced Eric the King of
the empire*

And his first order was to get the priestess out of the prison

He said get the priestess out the prison and bring her here now

*The priestess came while smiling and said: Is it true that the
king has died?*

Eric: Yes, come and sit beside me:

He hold her hand and said: help me to fix everything.

The priestess said: I can never say no or delay your majesty.

King: What do you want me to do?

The priestess said: you know what I want. The King's daughter.

King Eric said: guards, bring Walter daughter here and put his wife in jail.

They went looking for his wife, and found her crying over her husband, and they put her in jail.

They searched for the girl and did not find her.

King Eric ordered the guards to search for her in the entire city Her maid told the guards about the place where she is hiding, she was in the wine store and guards dragged her to King Eric. And she was Screaming: Father Father Mother Mother

When the priestess saw her she stood up and said: welcome baby I wanted to see you long time ago and she was examining her body. And touch her breast to check that she became adult.

The Girl: Go away what are you doing

The priestess turned to the king and shook her head and said while smiling, she is the third one

The king's daughter screamed: where is my father where is my father

The priestess laughed and said: Your father has died and laughed louder saying, but I did not revenge yet.

King Eric said: Put her in jail with the rest of the girls, and do not ever let anyone see them. Just give them food and drink

They drag her to jail, she does not know what will happen she was crying

King Eric told Tessa the priestess: What are you going to do now

She said, you will see, I will never disappoint you, the empire will return as powerful as it was before in one condition, is to do what I tell you to.

The priestess get nearer to King Eric and stepped above him on the throne, she kissed him and said you will see what I will do.

The priestess stood up and said: I have to go now, I have work to do and I want guards for protection and a Messenger in my house

King Eric said: ok, you have it.

The priestess went out while she was very happy because she is free now.

Village

The guards ran: Your majesty the army is coming

And Andre got shocked because there are only few shots have left.

He woke up of his bed and took a painkiller pill.

Andre told them Get ready and they took their places while he rose up to see the coming army

Ii was an army holding white flags, they stood in front of the gate and they dropped their weapons and threw them in front of the gate. one of them take some steps forward and said we are the emperor's army we dissented from him and we left our people, children and wives to join you, in the past two days we saw what we could never imagine, this is not human act but a God like you.

We are at your service, do whatever you like, if you want to cut our heads, if you want us to return back, or if you want we can join you to the war until the last soldier. And they all knelt to him.

Andre looked to Yamen the head of the village and say: what to do

Yamen said : you are the King

Andre said: Open the doors let them enter

Yamen said: Be careful perhaps someone wants to steal your magic stick and I will double the guards on your tent.

Andre said: Do whatever you want.

They celebrate all that night and one of them went to meet Andre

He asked Andre: shall we attack or wait for them to start? We are stronger than them, we have a king like you, who can destroy the entire empire.

Andre said: We will wait till tomorrow to see what will happen, then the soldier left.

He was sitting alone thinking what he would do if any developments happen? What if things got worse?

Then Jessey Entered and asked him if he needs anything and checked the wound in his shoulder. Andre was in very bad mood thinking.

She told him: What's wrong with you? I can see you worry

He said: Yes, a little

She asked him: Are you worried that this could be a plot from the king?

He said: No I'm thinking beyond that

He was hesitated to tell her the truth

She said: How come you worry and you have such an army, Oh my darling, come outside and see your army, we are stronger than them, now think about the throne, there are thousands waiting for somebody to save them from oppression. Some of them had come, some stayed idle others in prisons, and more and more..

Go outside and look at this great army that deserves to be proud of, all of them want to sacrifice for you.

He said: ok then, after my wound heals we will go to the empire

She smiled and said: My darling is so brave, He never fear anyone.

She hugged and kissed him saying do you love me?

He said: get your head down my shoulders and listen to my

heart beats, what he answered?
She puts her ears on his heart, and heard very quick heart
beating
She smiled and looked at him saying, I only heard your
heartbeats
He said: every beat is saying I love you, she gave him a hug and
they made love.

Empire

The priestess Tessa sent a stooge to the Hill's Valley to spy on them
and tell her about the news and the secret of that man.
She began preparing the oblation that she was waiting for long time.
Two weeks later the King Eric was concerned, nothing changed, the
army is dissident.
The king sent a messenger to the priestess asking about news.
She told the Messenger: Tell the king that everything will end after
midnight, there will be an extreme earthquake the ground of the
entire empire will shake everyone will feel it, even people in Hill's
Valley and it's sound will wake everybody up even animals.
The priestess ordered guards to bring the 3 girls to the temple (The
King's daughter, the blacksmith daughter and the orphan girl)
She took off the girls clothes and chained their hands from behind
and blocked their eyes and made then stand in front of the flying
snake statue.
She began to say her spell it was a long spell then frightening voices
starts to be heard, the more she talk the louder the frightening voices
get louder, very strong thunder and lighting, A Strong storm stroked
and the girls were screaming of fear.
She was shouting loud: Oh God save us, You are our Lord and our
protecting guard please honor us and accept this oblation she took
out the knife, and started with the blacksmith daughter then the
orphan girl then the king's daughter, she slayd them, blood dripped

toward the flying Serpent statue.

*The priestess bowed towards the statue saying oh lord save us from
the strange man, she was shivering and say please accept this
oblation from us.*

*Suddenly a very strong earthquake rocked the entire city, even
animals felt it and all people in Hill's valley woke up on fear, people
were wondering what this sound is?*

*King was so nerves that the plan may fail, and when he heard the
sounds and felt the earthquake, the King Eric stood up and raise the
glass of wine and said: Long live our Gods*

Hill's Valley

*Andre was sleeping he dreamed that he is sitting on a throne in a
Palace, and his mother and father are in front of him in the middle of
the hall bowing to him and there was a black star sign under them.
He got down from the throne and shouted mom dad and he ran to hug
them, then an earthquake shakes the star and brake it, his mother fall
down and his father remained cling to prevent himself from falling,
Andre said dad and ran to help him up he hold his hands to get him
up then a huge scary snake came from beneath him came out opened
its mouth and put half of the father inside it and dragged him to the
bottom, He screamed dad then he saw his mother and father and his
friends Ricardo and Vallen down there, the snake was eating them
one after another he screamed then he got up from the dream on the
voices of people screaming and Jesse was scared, crying and holding
her daughter Sophia, It was midnight.*

*Andre said: What is happening?, she says, I do not know something
rocked the whole country and our house, she was so afraid and asked
him, have you felt it?*

*He answered No, then he recalls the dream earthquake that shook his
father and mother and said yes yes I felt it, He went outside to the*

guards and asked them what happens
One guard answered: I do not know your majesty, everything had
shaken in the city
Andre Said: does anyone got hurt?
The Guard answered: Yes your majesty two people got injured after
their house collapsed.
He went to see the injured people, and then got back to bed.

He was asleep and in the morning, he open his eyes and saw a black
copra standing on its tail walking towards him, it attacked him biting
his finger firmly, he cried out and caught it from the back, dragged it
and push it to the wall.
He was screaming oh my hands, my hands
Jesse screamed oh my daughter, He saw Sofia on the floor crying
Jesse ran and hugged her daughter, oh baby Are you okay?
He says what happened! He did not understand what happened.
The Guards came inside, Andre told them there is a snake, shouting
and holding his finger there is a lack snake. They looked everywhere
but they didn't find any snake.
Andre holds Jesse's hands and told her, what happened
Jesse said: I sent my daughter to wake you up and she held your
finger and you looked at her then shouted and you caught my
daughter and dragged her and pushed her to hit the wall, you were
screaming holding your finger.

Andre Told her I'm sorry it was a dream like reality I have never
dreamed like this before.
He held Jesse's hands and said I'm sorry, I didn't mean to hurt your
daughter, I'm a little tense and he hugged the little Sophia.
Jesse said will bring you something to eat and prepare you a drink to
calm you down. Then she left.

A week later, Andre was very tired every night he wake up sweat and screaming from bad dreams while Jesse never left him alone, she sleeps beside him.

People and guards knew that he was ill and guards got used to it, He didn't sleep well at night

He was telling Jessey that he has terrifying dreams, snakes running after him and dogs eating his flesh.

Sometimes Andre cries while sleeping

Another week has passed, Andre is not getting better. He couldn't sleep well, He remained awake except for only an hour or two, and he was getting so tired.

One day, Andre was sleeping at morning, a strange person has entered the room, his eyes were scary, has hair on his face, looks like a snake face with red eyes, Andre feared him a lot and took out his gun quickly from under the bed, the man holds Andre's hands, Andre wanted to call the Guards but the man put his hands on Andre's neck he wanted to suffocate him, Andre was about to die, but he tried to push his hands away from his throat, He was about to die, he wanted to call the guards for help but he couldn't speak, He tried so hard to get a gun and stretched out his arms and took the gun, the man was pressing on his throat strongly, He was about to stop breathing and die, but in the last moment he shot him in head, Andre then fell on the floor, out of breath, coughing and trying to call for guards, then guards entered his room, and people gathered to see what had happened, Andre stood up and raise his hands to the guards signing to take Sophia away, as she was crying after hearing the shooting sound, there was a piece of bread in her little hands.

The guards standing at the door there was blood everywhere on the floor. after he stood up while guards didn't move he noticed that the one who had murdered was Jessey, his hands shivered, tears were running from his eyes, he fell on her body while shouting out loud No. He hugged her while crying like a child, And Sofia was beside her so afraid crying Mama Mama...

Guard were wonder what had happened:

One guard who was standing on the door said: my mistress (Jesse) ordered me to stay beside her daughter Sophia, she was eating bread and the king was burbles while sleeping as usual, he was shaking and crying but after few minutes he put his hands on his throat, choking himself, I was calling him trying to wake him up, His eyes were red looking at the sky, I was afraid that something bad may happen, I ran to My mistress Jessey calling for help, she was preparing water the water, I told her what had happened and she ran quickly to the room finding Andre killing himself, She held his hands to prevent him from suffocating himself, she was trying to wake him up, she asked me to get the doctor and after I got out of the room I heard the sound of that magic stick.

Andre cried: Get out all of you, I don't want to see anybody here, get out of the room, cried Andre.

People gathered outside of the room, they were saying that the King got mad, and some said that he suffered from fever and some said that she wanted to steal him then.

He stayed all night in his room crying nobody enters the room, And in the morning, he ordered soldiers to get him a horse and a carriage, He put her inside and took Sophia with him and said: Dear people Please gather and listen to me, as you can see that I'm so ill to the extent that I could never imagine, and because of this illness I wrongly killed .... He stopped talking and wept then he continued saying, I'm not here for war, not to become a king, I'm here for a job that I have to finish.

Stand for your land, don't give up to be humiliated and oppressed, You are strong now, no one can beat you, Gods bless you

He get on the horse back and Sophia with him, out of the sudden the blacksmith shouting please your majesty take me with you.
 Andre put his hands on the blacksmith shoulders and said: look behind you they need you more than me, I can rely on myself and I will raise my daughter.

please your majesty, take me with you, I can make swords and shields for you, I am a clever blacksmith, I will never forget what you had done to the king, you revenged to me , I owe you, your majesty, we all love you and wish you a quick recovery and to be back soon.

Blacksmith said: can I hug you, your majesty?, it may be the last time we meet.

" The blacksmith hugged him and gave him a shield and said: "I've made this for you"

Andre said: "thank you" and left.

He went to the place where Jessey's husband Aleksandro was buried and he dug a hole beside her husband and he was holding Sofia she was crying all this time. She was looking to the right and to the left, she thought she may see her mother and saying mum, mum

Andre he waited for her till she slept in order not to see her mother being buried. The girl slept and her tears were on her cheeks

He put her on the ground and carried Jessey and put her in the grave and he speaks to her before burying her "I am responsible for your daughter as long as I am alive. forgive me" then he looked to the sky and said "forgive me please God and wash my sin I didn't intend to do this and you best know "he was trembling and crying, his tears were on her grave, He buried her and sat on her grave and said:"yesterday, you were in my place and I was wondering what is the secret of that love? And I knew the meaning of love. He kissed her grave and got up then said come on, my daughter I have a mission that should be done before I die and they completed their way to the pyramid shaped mountain.

The empire

A messenger came and whispered words to the priestess. The priestess ran to the palace and entered while King Eric was sitting she told him while laughing : my love

King Eric said: I can see you pleased today, is there any good news?

The Priestess said: I always have good news that pleases you.

And she stood to kiss him, she was rubbing her nose with his and said: he killed his beloved and escaped from the Hill's village and now he is suffering.

The king : really?

The king was very happy with this news.

Priestess said: I have promised you to return your empire again as it was before but in one condition, to be the vice king

King Eric said: how?! I can't do this, the senate may disagree and this is against the laws of ruling the empire, you know that ruling here is only for our family.

Tessa asked him: who is the king here and who make orders ?

He said "I "

She said "well what is the problem, leave it all for me"

The king said "and what shall I do now? You should wait for my order

After one day, Tessa went hurrying to the king ,she said "It is time, get a writer and a messenger"

King Eric smiled and said "why are we waiting? Let's attack them now, the man who frightens us has gone.

She said "no, we are pressed for the army, war is useless now, she continued: do you know how many soldiers remained? The empire needs a great army to protect"

The king said: so send 5000 soldiers to kill Andre

She said: leave this for me ,he is suffering and dying slowly, Dear put it all on me for one condition is to appoint me as your vice king after everything returned back to what it was before. You know me well. King said "well when the army and the empire get back, I will declare you as my vice king to the senate.

The priestess ordered the writer saying: write down what I dictate you.

He wrote what she said. The king got annoyed from the letter and said "this is surrender and it is so humiliating for me.

The priestess Tessa said: Do not worry, I told you to leave it all for me, this is their opportunity to be saved from murder.

The messenger went to The Hill's Valley

The Hill's Valley

The Messenger: O people (they all gathered) I have a message for you from King Eric.

It says: From the empire to The Hill's Valley: I am king Eric the new king, King Walter had died and all his evil had gone, he killed many innocent people and dislodged mothers and children because of his war and I was against this war and I advices him to negotiate, but king Walter's ego and pride led us to what we are now distributed. And I obliged not to raise any war against my people and the empire gates are opened, welcoming you ,come back to your families and children, we do not want more killing from today on, we want to live with dignity and freedom. Whoever wants to live here is accepted.

We want to reunite, we do not want any distinction, we want to live in the same family as one man and I pledge in front of you and god to defend what's right and diffuse what's wrong. And this message is an endorsement from King Eric, the King of the empire.

The messenger gave them the letter and returned.

People and guards gathered: is this a trap to destroy us?! some of them believed and others didn't, and one of them said: Hey, people we do not have a king now and our king left, but what about sending some soldiers to make sure of it.

Some soldiers went to the empire, they found opened gates and as if nothing had happened and there were welcoming people, they gave them food and drink and they were happy by their return. every now and then a group returns back to the empire ,no one remained in the Hill's valley except, the blacksmith, old people, some patients and some people who got used to live in this village, king Yamen said "I am very old now ,I will live the rest of my life here and I will die here.

Empire

After the army returned to the empire, It became powerful as it was before, the priestess Tessa asked king Eric to keep his promise and assign her as the vice king

King Eric said "I will meet the senate today and we will see their opinion

The priestess said: and I will attend this meeting

King Eric summoned the senate and said "I congratulate you for returning our empire as it was, thanks to Tessa and I have appointed her the vice king.

Their elder one Pabl got angry, he said: what are you saying your majesty, you know judging rules and we will not allow this to happen

King said: but Tessa helped us and we got the army back, she did what king Walter was not able to do and without any lose

Tessa entered and told Pabl : can you reject the king's order

Pabl answered: yes, I reject and I will not allow this to happen

Tessa got out a knife and slaughtered him, he fell on the table

And she said: this is the punishment of disobeying the king's orders "the senate looked at the king ,waiting for his reaction against her, but the king said: is there anyone disagree? Then they left their chairs without opposition.

After a month, the priestess Tessa came to the king ,she said "I want to prepare an oblation to god"

he looked at her and said "why then is the oblation for, Andre is almost dead according to what you said, he has gone mad and escaped and Hill's valley will be under our control "

She said "the oblation is effective only for 3 months and it does not last and he may return and ruin us.

the king said "and how can we find virgin girls you know we are not able to find a girl except the king's daughter, I do not think it is time now, also we have a great army, we can search for him everywhere and kill him, I will attack the Hill's valley and kill them all till they tell me where he is?"

The priestess said "then, do what you want but do not come back and ask for my help"

the king said "we would not lose anything if we attacked them "he continued "I do not want him to find any place hide or to protect him and if he returned after sometime , he will not find the village as it was before, I want to demolish this village I want only the empire to remain,

The priestess Tessa said "you will do like what king Walter did before, when he did not do what I told him to, and he destroyed everything" and she got angry and went out.

The king said to the messenger "go secretly to see how many soldiers left in their army.

" The messenger went and after 3 days he came back and said "there are no one except old people, the blacksmith, children and fifty guards.

King said: I will prepare 1000 soldiers to force them to tell us where is Andre or kill them all. King Eric addressed them and said "do not leave anyone alive in the village, kill the old and the young" and search for Andre and the little girl.

The priestess entered the palace, she was very angry, she told the king: Do you think that what you are doing will destroy him?, please leave him to me

King said: no I will send my soldiers everywhere to search for him , and I will get rid of him

The priestess said "do what you want",

The king sent the army, there was no strong resistance, they entered the village and killed the rest of guards and dominated the village .they caught their ruler "Yamen" and asked him "where did Andre go and the young girl who was with him? "Yamen answered "I do not know, he killed jessey and took the young girl with him and went away from here, they slaughtered him, and they asked one following the other, when they not answer soldiers slaughter them no one replied except one man, he said "Andre was asking about the pyramid shaped mountain and there is a cave in it, he may be living there" and the soldiers asked him "where is the pyramid shaped mountain?" and then they also slaughtered him, they executed all people who were in the village , no elder nor young remained, they got out and went to search for the pyramid shaped mountain and they found a horse and they searched for him there but they did not find him.

And after few days, they returned back to the king and told him: "we have killed all people in the village and they told us that (King Andre and his daughter) are in the pyramid shaped mountain, we found their horse, but we neither find Andre nor the girl.

The king got very angry,

Tessa the priestess entered and said "he will teach the girl his magic and she will become more powerful than him, I have warned you and you did not listen to me.

King Eric said: and what is the solution, what to do now? Don't say that you want more girls, we cannot find any.

The priestess laughed and said "no, is there anything more lovable and beautiful than offering a baby to god.

King Eric looked at her and shouted: "impossible, it is dangerous " he said "let me think it is very difficult to take a baby from his family. The priestess said: it is not that difficult, leave it to me, I only want one baby.

the king said "well, but quickly" the priestess went and took some soldiers with her she entered every home, searching for a baby ,she found one, she took him from his parents, his father took a sword and lifted it at the priestess's face and the guards killed him and the baby's mother was crying why are you taking my baby?

The priestess said "it is the king's order". Do you want to die or let us take the baby?, she took him to her house, many people protested against the king and they went to the palace to take the baby back to his mother But the king didn't listen or care for them. The senate came to meet the king and they asked him "how can you allow killing an innocent baby under your protection".

* The king said "are you protesting now?, but you did not protest for the girls, you agreed then, what had changed you?" do you want us to die, and lose our army? This is just a baby and his parents will forget him soon and will have others, I do not want anyone to discuss it, this is for the empire's safety. The meeting ended "the king sat down and he felt some guilt about his decision concerning the baby, but it is useless, no time for regret. After the moon had went*

out, the priestess Tessa started to prepare the oblation for the flying snake god, she was reading books and there was a thunder sound and strong wind voice of the baby crying, she took the knife and slaughtered him then cried and said "accept this oblation" and she prostrated to the statue and said "I want to be the queen of the empire".

King Eric felt a tremor in his body, he went to sleep and in the morning ,he got up finding his body swollen and he became so ill suffering from smallpox, he stayed ill in bed for a month, the priestess requested to make quarantine for the king because his illness is infectious.

There is a law in the empire that says "anyone has an infectious disease, should be burnt"

And after days Tessa decided to burn the king because this disease is infectious and may kill thousands of citizens she burnt him and she became the queen of the empire.

Abdicate Andre

Andre and Sophia went to the Pyramid shaped mountain. They came down from the horse to mislead the soldiers.

Andre carried Sophia and went to the Spaceship. She got used to him and over time she forgot her mother. He worked on trying to connect electricity to the spaceship in order to launch the satellite rocket.

Sophia called him "Dad" and he loved her so much and was responsible for her he taught her everything, he taught her the bible and she became Christian where nobody on this land were Christian except the 2 of them .

78

When sleeping, Andre was tying himself with the belt because he was watching nightmares every day; he was seeing Jessie in his terrifying dreams.

Empire

Tessa the priestess became the Queen. She has jailed all the members of Senates lest they turn against her. She killed all persons less than 50 and jailed all persons more for lifelong. Tessa was afraid of Andre and Sophia so much. She sent soldiers monthly to look for them in vain. She did not care a lot for Andre as she knew that he gone made; she believed that he will die of sorrow. Tessa, thought to make a great oblation to eliminate the child. However, she did not know the child's name or age, moreover, she has never seen her before; and the oblations do not work without enough information. Soldiers failed to find Andre and the child so Tessa thought they were dead. Tessa was lonely, so she decided to marry in order to have children who would inherit the governance after she would die. One day, She saw one of the guards whose name was Roy; he was so handsome that she admired him. She let him enter her palace; she offered to marry him. She tempted him with ministry and money. She said that she wanted some honest person to help her govern the empire. He agreed in the case although she was 8 years elder. She made a great wedding party and after one month she became pregnant.

Roy was responsible for the kingdom. He solved the problems of the people while Tessa cared for great problems which Roy could not solve.

After Tessa gave birth to her baby, Victor, she decided to make a wealth for him. She raised taxes on people and she imposed taxes on soldiers after there were no taxes on military members. People were angry especially the poor. The queen ordered guards to gather persons who cannot pay taxes to share in establishing a statue for

79

her and ordered also to execute in the field whoever refuses her orders.

After 9 years, Sophia became 11 and Andre became 54 years old. Sophia got used to Andre 's frightening dreams.

Andre worked hard to finish what he started a very long time ago. He spent all the time seeking the problem, examining wires and disjoining the cabin. Suddenly, he found a separated electronic board because of the crash. He was very happy for that. He installed the board well and then he started to turn on the power but it did not work. He was certain that the circuit is ok. After several trials he became desperate. Andre decided to devote his efforts to teach the girl. He taught her reading and writing and she was intelligent so she understood science well and quickly. She asked him all the time about many things and he answered her in details. He told her his full and true story; how and why he was there and everything about his life. He did not lie except in one thing; he told her that when he came there, he met her mother and got married and then her mother died after she gave birth to her.

Sophia became 14 years old. She became brilliant and Andre taught her one lesson every day. He also learnt her shooting, Karate, physics, chemistry and many other things.

One day, while Sophia was playing, she found the i-pad of Vallin in his memories fund. She went to Andre saying: "Dad, what is this?" Andre told her about Vallin, and after she insisted to know how it works, Andre tried to turn it on, laughing at her innocent intelligence.

Andre took the charger and went down to the central battery in order to connect wires for charge.

He remembered that a machine that generates energy does not work with one battery, it needs two; however, the second battery has been missed in Hill's Valley when he was launching a missile upon the king during the war.

Andre hesitated to go there. He was afraid of being killed. He did not know what has happened to people there, it was too long time.

After the i-pad was charged, Andre gave it to Sophia and they played with it together. Andre cried when he watched his friends' photos as they were young on the ipad, and Sophia watched the photos, too.

Few days after that, he was teaching Sophia an influential lesson, it was about 'Mother'. He was confused and hesitated. While he was explaining Mothers' roles in educating their children and their roles in society, he suddenly looked to Sophia who was crying and wondering: "Dad, where is my mother? I miss her. Where did she die?". He replied: "It is time to tell you the truth".

He planned to go to visit the tomb of Sophia's mother then bring the battery in order to make the last trial. He looked for the horse but he found that it was killed by an arrow. There was no way but walking. He took some bullets and walked with the girl, sometimes he carried her because she was unable to walk. He also got tired because he became old.

They reached Sophia's mother's tomb, Andre said: "This is your mother's tomb". She cried at the grave and after she calmed down she asked: "Dad, whose grave is this?" Hardly, he answered: "It is your dad's". She looked at him with amazement crying: "What do you say? Who are you?" Shaking his head he replied "No". Sophia was shocked and she became very sad.

The girl sat down distracted between the tombs of her parents; she took some sand to put it on the tombs alternately. She spent half a day shocked greatly and indulged in sorrow. She was crying and talking to herself. Andre was very sad for Sophia; he tried to approach to her by holding her hands but she went away and looked angrily to him saying: "Stay away from me. You were cheating me all the time, I thought you were my dad"
 Andre : I told you that your mother is dead.

Sophia: you did not tell me that my father is dead. Instead you took his place.

Andre : It was wrong to do that but I wanted to compensate you for father's love. I didn't want you to feel like an orphan. Come with me, my baby.

Sophia: "No, leave me alone. I want to die here with my parents".

Andre : "Are you crazy! Father who keeps not who beget. I who educated and protected you, I who saved you and your mother's lives"

Sophia: "It does not matter. Why did not you tell me about my mother's tomb and my father's truth?"

Andre :" You were too young to understand. How could I tell you the truth as you were a child? Now you know where they are. They are dead. Is there any change?"

Andre sat down in front of Sophia and said: "I promised your mother to care for you as long as I'm alive." She looked to him asking: "How did you save our lives?"

He told her the whole true story. And when Sophia asked him about the reason of their departure from Empire, he told her the story of Alekhandro (her father) and what happened to him.

82

Sophia looked to Andre and asked: "How did my mother die? And who did bury her here?"

Andre sat down a bit and then he cried. He was unable to talk but separate and uncompleted words then he said: "There are many things that you don't understand" She replied insisting on knowing what had happened: "I am not stupid nor young"

Andre touching her cheeks: "No, baby, you are not, however, your mother's death was mysterious. I will tell you the truth, in a condition that you come with me now. Please, don't make me regret for telling the truth. I want to educate you until I die, please baby"

Sophia: "Don't say 'baby'. I'm not your baby. Well, I'll go with you in a condition that you tell me the reason of my mother's death"

Andre shake his head agreeing to her and promising to tell her the truth soon. Sophia stood up and walked with Andre holding his hand and while walking she asked him again about the truth and if he wanted to tell her while they were walking, but he advised her not to rush asking for a lead time to think about how could he tell her everything. He stopped and put his hands on her shoulders saying: "Listen, I promise to tell you everything after we would comeback from Hill's Valley as we will take something from there, and please, don't speak with anybody"

They continued walking to the village and as soon as they have arrived, they got astonished at the sight. The village was completely destroyed and dead bodies spread all over the place, corpses were crucified. Sophia screamed when she saw killed and burnt children; their bodies were rotting. Andre asked Sophia to close her eyes and carried her then hurried looking for the battery. When he got into his room, he remembered the accident, and suddenly, they saw a crying trembling old woman saying: "Please, don't kill me"

83

Andre : "Don't be afraid. Is there anybody here?"

The old woman crying: "No, there is not"

Andre : "What happened to the village?"

The old woman looked at him and started crying. He came closer and hugged her and so did Sophia.

Andre : "Calm down. What happened?"

The old woman: "Many years ago, the king ordered to kill all of us"

Andre : "Was not there army to protect you and the village?"

The old woman: "Yes, there was, but 8 or 10 years before, a messenger came and declared reconciliation and all of the soldiers returned back to Empire. Just me and few persons who accustomed to live here stayed. And one day while sleeping they attacked us and killed whoever they saw"

Andre : "How did you escaped?"

The old woman: "I was hiding in a will when I heard them carefully asking about someone called Andre and killing whoever doesn't know him. Somebody said that after Andre killed his beloved, he took her and the little child and ran way"

Sophia screamed

The old woman: "What's the matter with you, dear?"

Sophia was crying and screaming. She asked the old woman: "Do you know the names of the child or the killed woman?"

The old woman: "The mother's name was Jessie; however I don't know her child's name."

Andre was shocked. He tried to explain the truth to Sophia but she didn't listen. She screamed and cried to keep him away from her.

Andre : "I promised to tell you the truth"

Sophia: "I already knew the truth"

She cried hugging the old woman, Emilia, and saying: "He is not human; he is savage as he killed my mother".

They spent two days in Hillside village. Sophia was crying all the time. She didn't look at Andre. Moreover, she screamed in his face every time he tried talking to her or even come near to her. She repeated: "I want to go to my parents' grave".

Andre was sleeping; he was watching frightening dreams as usual. The old woman was afraid of him and she awakened him many times, but Sophia told her to let him dream as he always do that; "That because of what he did to my mother" said Sophia.

Andre spent two days trying to convince Sophia and Emilia to return back with him to the spaceship because it was too dangerous to stay in Hill's Valley as it was expected for them to be killed any time.

Emilia: "We should go with him for the sake of ourselves; I will be with you like your mother".

Finally, Sophia agreed in a condition that he would not talk to or deal with or order her.

Andre agreed on the Sophia's condition. He looked for the battery until he found it in a chicken coop and also he found a horse but with no cart. The old woman rode the horse and Sophia returned back walking besides Andre. The girl wanted to go to her parents' tombs and she already did. By the road, they stopped to visit the tombs; she sat down there for some time and then she wiped her tears saying: "Let's go."

Andre , Sophia, and Emilia keep walking until they reached the spaceship. The sun was about to rise up. The old woman entered the spaceship. She did not believe what she saw. She said: "Wow! Impossible! I don't believe that you who made this. It cannot be a human work. The old woman wandered in the spaceship, she couldn't believe what she saw; she was amazed.

Sophia went to her bed trying to take some rest as she was very tired because she did not sleep well for two days.

 Andre hurried to settle the second battery. He went to control cabin in order to turn on power and suddenly, the engine was operated and lights were on. Emilia screamed: "Oh my God! What's happened?" Andre was whooping: "I did it, I did it". He hugged the old woman while he was crying of joy. The woman did not understand what he meant.

Sophia waked up dazed; she came out of her room. Andre rushed to her: "My daughter…" Andre said, but she got away from him saying: "Stay away from me".

The old woman was watching in amazement. Lights were on everywhere.

Andre hurried to instructions' book reading and following instructions, pressing on the buttons trying to launch the rocket. Whenever he tried to press launch button, he heard a crackling sound coming from the upper part of the spaceship. He was disappointed. He climbed up the spaceship to see what caused the crackling sound.

He found a large tree branch blocking the launch slot. He tried to break it but he could not. He decided to try it again the next day. He went to bed, tied himself with the belt and slept.

Suddenly, while sleeping, he felt someone walking towards him. He thought it was a dream but he found Sophia putting the gun on his head. "Sophia, my child, what are you doing? Please, don't kill me today, please, if you want, kill me tomorrow" Andre said to Sophia who was crying and shaking his head saying: "No, I know that you want to bring your people to our land in order to destroy it like yours. I'm not stupid".

Andre : "No, baby, we'll teach you and transfer our knowledge and technology to your land. We will save the efforts of 1000 years in few years; hospitals, education, safety, electricity, transportation, equality... etc. Are you satisfied with your unjust governor?"

Sophia: "He is unjust but it's better to be followed by a good one. You want to steal our land and fight us with your weapons. You will spread miss. Look at this weapon (the gun); I became stronger than you, the strong is strong and the weak is weak".

Andre realized that it was his fate. He begged to her: "Please, kill me now and bury me with your mother"

"No, you don't deserve that" Sophia replied "you should be crucified" and shot him many times to revenge her mother then she fell to the ground crying. The old woman walked up to the sound of the bullets; she hurried to Sophia who was on the ground crying, she hugged the girl saying that he deserved that.

Emilia and Sophia went to bed and in the morning, Sophia pulled his body out of the spaceship; she brought some wood and crucified it"

When Emilia saw the crucified corpse, she asked Sophia to stop doing that: "Oh dear! He is dead now and he deserves that, why do you crucify him?" Emilia said.

Sophia: "It is not enough. I have revenged for my mother and I will revenge for my father too".

The pyramid shaped mountain

Two years passed after Andre's death. Sophia and the old lady (Emilia) lived together, she even called her: " mother" . They lived in the spaceship and she was reading books and learning. From time to time she go to visit the tombs of her dead mother and father scattering flowers upon them.

One day when she was in a visit to her mother and father , a person called "Fred" saw her, he escaped from the Empire after being told that the tribute had been imposed . He was poor man without family neither kids nor wife. Fred was watching her scattering flowers upon the tombs of her mother and father wondering "Who would be that little girl? Why is she at such place alone? He was watching her and following her.

She left the place, walking at the opposite direction to the empire's way, he wondered, watched and followed her. at night she arrived to the place of the spaceship, he saw a strange thing, he saw the spaceship glittering with lights from inside, he was dazzled by the view, he sat on the ground watching in hesitation and eventually he decided to leave. Fred returned again to The Empire.

The Empire.

He hurried to the gates of the palace, asking to meet the queen. The guards mocked at him and said: "Nobody is able to meet the queen. He said:" It is serious I beg you" .The guard said: "wait a minute, I'll tell the minister", he hurried to the minister (Roy) and told him that someone wanted to meet the queen with important news" . "Let him in" replied the minister. Fred entered and the minister (Roy) asked him: "what are this news that you have? What is your story?" Fred sat down and began to tell the story. When he finished the minister couldn't believe him but he said: " If you are lying you'll be executed and if you are telling the truth you'll be awarded by 500 golden pieces from the queen".

Fred accepted the provisions and the minister sent ten guards with him to guide them to the place. The queen Tessa entered and the minister kissed her hands and asked for Victor. Where is he now?

She replied :"He is playing, he has become nine years old now" she said. "Are there any news about the statue?" she asked.

He answered her:" They are working hard on it but there is a person who has told me a strange story of a girl that he have seen, she is living in a pile of iron which emitting lights from inside at night.

The Queen was astonished she shouted at his face: " When, where have you seen him, and where is he now?" she asked." your majesty, I have sent him with ten guards to prove that his story is real". "You are stupid" she said" why didn't you tell me from the beginning?

"I wasn't sure so I didn't like to tell you till I prove that he saying the truth" he answered."

That is the Andre's place and the child that I have been searching for all these years long" she said

"Woe to you, why only ten why haven't you sent ten thousand , twenty thousand or all the army, has he told you where the place is?

"Roy said:" No but I only sent ten of the guards with him to know the place" .The queen was raged.

He asked her: "Why are you so tense, it's just a girl and 10 Guards are fully able to destroy a girl.
She said to him:" Don't you know that man who killed more than 30, 000 soldiers alone and you send 10 soldiers? Perish 10 soldiers? So stupid are you. They own a miraculous magic stick that is able to kill all people. The queen asked: have he seen Andre?"
Minister Roy said:" No, he said that he had seen only a little girl."
Queen Tessa was so annoyed and waiting for news that she couldn't sleep.

The pyramid shaped mountain

It was midnight, Sophia and Emilia were sleeping. The army arrived at the place and was astonished when they saw the spaceship, the lights were off.

One of them said "I don't see any lights, let's approach to make sure if anyone lives inside."

They approached walking and looking for the entrance and Fred led them to the entrance where the girl had entered but the door was locked.

One of them tried to open it, but he couldn't as the door was closed, he took a stick and tried to open the door, but to no avail. He ship

The Earth

They received the signal of the satellite. Happiness spread all over the world for this news about new life and a land full of treasures. The scientists and the whole world became so eager for that great project. One of the scientists (Robin Adam) was afraid of two expectations; the signals may come as a result of explosions inside the ship and the satellite may have been launched to one of the galaxies and began to send signals or that the satellite May have been already in its planned place but there is a problem in manufacturing such spaceships which may cost thousands of millions, also food and water for those who want to leave.

They decided to send the first group of people males and females but not more than 30 persons with their families; if the trial of this group succeeded, they will send a second one with a more developed satellite. Scientists had developed a very high technological satellite over those years, which is able to send voice calls to the new land and vice versa from there to our land? The scientists became so Ernest concerning that great project.

The hard work began in order to fulfill the project within few years, they decided to send 3 astronauts and 10 doctors to educate the children. The United States of America dedicated a sum of 10 billion dollars to support the project.

Next month the ship will be ready, with the names of volunteers.

After a month nobody submit the volunteering application except ; 14 persons from USA with their children , 7 from south Africa , 5 from south America , 8 from Japan and south Korea and 3 from Canada , with total of 37 persons and the list became as follows:

(1) 14 from USA

(2) 7 from South Africa

(3) 5 from South America

(4) 8 from Japan and South Korea

(5) 3 from Canada

They were enough to reproduce on that land. They were examined for their medical, fitness and standard of intelligence state. Also doctors and astronauts had been selected. And after 6 months the spaceship was ready with its full equipment and its crew. The American president awarded the volunteers and in the next day they were ready for launching. They left the earth in a great celebration and unprecedented broadcasting.

The countdown began 321 and the spaceship was launched, cameras recorded the scene till the ship became out of sight, going to the new land , the land of treasures.

The New Land

Sophia could no longer bear living alone; she should prepare herself for the coming of Andre's people. She sat and went in a deep thought of what would happen if she went to the empire. No one knows her, she was talking to herself:" Why do I live alone ?, what have I done to receive such severity being forced to leave" she decided to go to the empire. She took what she needed like food, the gun and some shots and buried the rest of the shots under a big rock, she moved towards the empire, she visited the tombs of her father and mother. She said:" Oh Mother and father help me to live at ease and prosperity and face Andre's people who treacherously killed my mother, I would never forget your revenge father, I shall take it from the king, I'll kill him, I promise you". "Farewell.. in a hope to visit you again Don't forget me in your prayers I love you.

She went towards the empire, it was afternoon, and people were at work. The gate was crowded with people. There were guards on the gate, she didn't want to enter alone to avoid the investigation of the guards who may examine her and take the gun. She knew well that they have no idea about the gun but they may take it from her. She waited and watched far away hoping that some people will come with whom she enters. A carriage with some people behind came. She crept and entered with them letting her hair down her face as she didn't want to pull their attention. She managed to enter.

93

She roamed in the city and the market. She had some feeding pills enough for only one day. She must find a way to live, either work or beg. She was beautiful she faced some harassment while she was walking in the market; some persons may offer her food for sex. She reached a shop and asked for work and he replied:" why are you searching for work? We shall all serve you and work for you, the whole shop is yours and the home too. She felt something strange in his words, she asked:"But how?" The man answered: "You marry me and all things become yours"

"No, thanks" she said and went out.

He said: "Think well I have made a big offer, it will last till the end of the night you will never find a better offer", he laughed and said:" Oh what a poor woman"

The sun began to set, people began to go to their homes and the bars began to open. At night she found herself in the capture of the drunk and city guards, she was able to defend herself but she was afraid that she might kill somebody and as a result, she may enter the prison and lose the gun. She may also stay all her life in prison. She was trying to disappear among buildings in order not to be seen by the drunk. She found a barn; she didn't find any other place so she slept her first night in. Next morning she was waking up hearing the sounds of animals and people, she recalled the shopkeeper's offer and felt remorse why she didn't accept the shopkeeper's offer. She stood and left her place. She crept so as not to be observed by anybody, she began to search for work, she searched everywhere, she found a person, seemingly rich, and she began to ask him for work." Yes "he said "I am looking for a girl who can clean the house where I live with my wife and children." He was looking at her body allover but she said:" Yes, when?" He answered "Now, come with me"

She was glad and went with him, he entered and said:" that is my home. She asked him: where your wife and kids are? He said" they have gone to see their grandmother , they will return after a while, Sophia said well I have to start cleaning before they come he said and I am going to my work they may come late as they missed their grandmother , I will return after sunset , I want you to clean well . He returned after sunset, he found her sitting beside the lamp, he asked: have my wife and my kids returned?"No" she said, he replied: "They may be on their way now".

He went to his room, he began to scatter his bed sheet and blanket, and then he went to her and said my room is untidy why haven't you clean it? She wondered and said no master I have cleaned and arranged it well. He said come and see by yourself. she went and saw the untidy room and said sorry master I may have forgotten to arrange this room, suddenly he pushed her to the bed , she resisted and said to him :"Go away" ,she tried to make him fear the coming of his wife and kids saying "Your wife will enter now, let's do this later, he laughed and said I have no wife and no kids, he tried to kiss her, she resisted strongly, she couldn't , she was crying, then picked the gun and shot him in stomach, he couldn't breathe. She was trembling she heard the neighbors going out of their homes, their voices were high, they were asking what was that sound, she stood up and went out through the window and cried. She escaped to the barn to sleep beside the horses She was weeping and saying: "Father and mother, I really missed your mercy and your protection" she looked at the sky and say "O GOD help me I am lost, I cannot do anything." She cried till she slept. And In the morning she found someone waking her up saying:" why you sleep here my

95

daughter? Where are your parents? She said:"I have no parents, they died.

He said "Do you have relatives?"

She answered: I am alone.

He said come with me and he took her hands, she was afraid he may do like what the man whom she killed yesterday did. She pushed his hands and said:" No, let me go. My God will not leave me. "He pitied on her so much. He said: come don't be afraid I will take care of you, he said " wait I will call my wife, he summoned his wife to the barn, his wife pulled her and said:" come my kid don't be afraid and she went with them. She felt somewhat comfortable and entered the house with them.

He said:" My name is Mark, my wife is Maria and that is Jasmine, my daughter. Mark told his wife:"give her some food, and I am going to search, I may find work this day. He left and she gave her some bread and some water and said "sorry we only have bread and water". Sophia said "never mind" after food she was playing with their young Jasmine all day. Mark retuned, greeted them and sat down, he was angry somewhat, his wife asked him "Have found any work today? He shook his head and said "tomorrow things will get better, and God will grant us. Sophia said:"I can work .He said:"No my kid, working at such age may cause problems to you "He asked his wife is there enough food till tomorrow? She said yes we have enough food for 2 days.

While she was sleeping at her first night she heard a quarrel between the man and his wife. She said "we don't have enough food to feed this girl? I didn't want to tell you so in front of her" He said" Tomorrow will be better, don't worry, God will grant us .I will sell the horse tomorrow and there will be enough money to feed us for a month.

Next day. He returned home with no money. She asked him "Have you sold your horse? He said nobody bought it, they said it is old; they offered a low price and I refused to sell at that low price. Tomorrow I will again look for work.

Mark said:"I heard that a thief broke into our neighbor house and killed him. Lock the doors well and the guards are everywhere, he may fall in their hands.

When they went to sleep there was the same quarrel

Maria said "That girl has come with poverty, how will I feed my daughter, we have no food" Her voice was high this time

He said "Tomorrow God will grant us, things will get better". When Mark got up in the morning he didn't find Sophia in her bed, he looked for her but he didn't find her. Maria, his wife said "Now you will have money the cause of poverty has left". He was angry and went to look for her.

Sophia didn't want to live humiliated, she decided to live at her place, her home, where nobody bothers her, she hunts what she likes. She said that solitude is better than merciless people, she wanted to live among them but it was her destiny to live alone.

She was afraid, ten guards were standing on the gate, they were investigating people who get in or out because of the murder accident. She waited for a chance to go out. Suddenly she saw many horses came near to the gate, they were about to go out. She said I will go out with them. She approached the gate waiting them to pass. She moved beside them and at the gate she went out with them.

She has been set free now, suddenly someone said "stop" they stopped all and Sophia froze out of fear. Someone got down and said oh you girl come, she was trembling, she went toward him and said "yes, master" where are you going alone? she didn't answer ,he repeated his question , she shook her head and said I don't know where am I going I don't have any one, he wondered and said where are your parents? She said they are dead I don't have a family.

He said: what is your name?

"Sophia" She said,

He said; come with me I will introduce you to my mother.

She said: I beg you, your majesty, let me go.

He held her hand and said; don't be afraid, do you know me?

"No" said she

He said: I am Victor, Son of the queen

She didn't believe but asked him" and where is the king?"

He looked at her and said "the king! He died of a malicious disease and my mother reigned after him"

She asked "Is he your father?

He said: no, come, let's talk. My mother will welcome you; he got one of the guards down of the horses back and let her ride, on the way she asked him why have you stopped?

He said I don't know something has attracted me to you; I would like to know who is that beautiful girl, why does she walk alone? Then I ordered guards to stop,

Sophia asked: where were you going Victor "I was going to hunt but now, I have changed my mind.

He let her enter the palace and said: "mother, come, I have got a surprise for you.

His mother entered, looked at her and said "who is that girl?" Victor got close to his mother and asked her in law voice: "mother please be good with her, she is beautiful, she has attracted me, and I like her"

His mother looked at him and left the hall,

He said to Sophia: "don't worry, this is my mother's attitude, come sit beside me, let us talk for few minutes,

they sat together and talked , he asked her about her parents, how did they die and she told him that she doesn't know anybody in the city and she live temporary with a kind family .

Victor ask servants saying " Bring all the food, we have an important guest" He continued "no, no, not a guest, but the wife of Prince Victor.

For the first time she feels shy, he was attractive like his father, and he was good at argument and persuasion like his mother.

They sat on the table and the queen Tessa was present at lunch but she didn't talk. Victor asked his mother "mother, what is your opinion?

The queen Tessa looked at her and went further on, eating. After they finished, Sophia went to wash her hands. She sat and arranged her hair, her clothes. Tessa said to Victor "when she come, let us be alone, I like to talk with her for a few minutes.

He approached towards his mother and said " Let me choose for myself mother, one time, if she goes, I will go with her, I beg you, she is nice I have loved her, don't you see how she is beautiful,

She said do you know who is she, who her parents are, or even her family, do you know anything about her? She continued, I want you to marry the noblest girl in the city, you are a prince and hundreds of girls wish you to be their husband.

He said "O are you taking about nobility? so my father origin is enough, all people talked about your marriage, he was so poor, he was a guard under your control, and you married him, what is the difference between you and me?

She said: "I had my reasons.

His father entered, he was administering the work in the statue. He has a strong character.

He said "father, I have found a beautiful girl today; I like to marry her, what is your opinion?

His father:" You should convince your mother, son"

he said:" mother either I marry her or escape with her or stay all my life without marriage."

She said well my son wash your hand now, and let me sit with her and talk.

The queen sat on her throne and Sophia entered. She asked "What is your name"

"Sophia" she answered.

Queen:"My son told me that you are an orphan, is this right?"

"Yes, your majesty" Sophia answered.

"Where was your father working?" asked the queen.

"I don't know but my grandmother told me, before she died, that he worked in the army"

She asked" How did he die?"

Sophia said:"He died at the annual party of the king".

The queen asked:" Do you have a family?"

She shook her head " no your majesty"

the queen stood up , left her throne and went towards Sophia, she took 500 golden pieces and threw them upon Sophia and said :" My little girl I know you are a beautiful girl and so many people would like to marry you , I also know that you are poor, but my son is a prince, take that money and live your life far from my son ,I want a suitable girl to marry him.

Sophia Said "Don't misunderstand me your majesty, I don't chase victor, he who stopped me on the way, I don't want any of this, I haven't come for money

The queen said "stop", I don't want to hear your story, and I didn't ask you about it ".

Sophia said ' thank you for your hospitality."

The queen said:"come and Take the money and stay away from my son, I don't want to see you again.

Victor was waiting out the door. He wanted to know what happened. He asked Sophia, she told him that his mother gave her money to leave him.

She said: I didn't want to take the money, but she forced me to, please tell your mother that I got the message and thank her for her hospitality: I will leave now"

Victor was angry "no stay, I beg you, I really loved you, I will marry you whatever happens, I will not allow others to interfere when it comes to my private life", you can take money, and it is yours now. She went out and he followed her, "Sophia I forgot to ask you where you live?

She said "I don't know where I live; I have no home I shall search for a new one"

Victor said " Listen, you have enough money to buy a new home now, I will meet you in front of the exit gate at the same place tomorrow and I will convince my mother, he holds her hands and said " will you promise me not to leave me" she nodded her head with yes.

He said to her:" Leave my mother on me".

She looked at the money and looked to the sky and said: thank GOD

She was angry about the behavior of the Queen Tessa.

She went to Mark's home, knocked at the door, it was opened and Mark asked her "where were you kid? We have searched for you every where".

Maria looked at her contemptuously.

Mark said:" Bring food for Sophia, she may be hungry".

"We have no food "said Maria.

Sophia said:"No thanks, I ate".

She took 50 golden pieces from her pocket and put them on the table.

Mark looked at the gold and said "Gold?" He looked at his wife Maria and said: "Haven't I told you that God will grant us.

His eyes were full of tears.

He hugged Sophia and said "Thanks my kid"

Maria couldn't believe what she saw.

Mark Said: "I will go to buy bread, milk and chicken".

Maria stood shy of her behavior towards Sophia. She came close to Sophia and sat beside her, Jasmine her daughter was laying on her shoulders. Maria said "I'm really sorry Sophia; you know that we

103

are so poor, sometimes we stay two days without food, and even my daughter I couldn't find food for her.

Sophia "I know, that is why I returned to give you some money"

Maria hugged Sophia while she was weeping and saying "we beg your pardon, you know poverty is a bad thing.

In the evening they sat together on the table to have dinner "Mark asked Sophia" From where have you got this money kid?"

She answered: "It is a grant of God, a strange thing happened to me today, I went out to search for work, then the Queen's son stopped me on my way, he asked about my name, he offered to take me home to meet his mother, I refused but he said that he is the son of the queen, I didn't believe him, but I went with him, he asked me to have lunch with him on the royal table and before I leave, the queen gave me money, and I returned here.

Mark asked "Have you met the queen? How? We've been trying to meet her since 2 years ago, and she refuses. But what did her son want from you?"

Sophia answered: "I don't know, but he said that he wanted to spend the rest of his life with me, I think he wants to marry me" Maria said: Beware of him, he may deceive you.

Sophia said: "don't worry about me. And after they finished launch Sophia said: I will go search for a house to buy.

Mark Said: Why do you search for a house, this is your home dear.

Sophia said: "I don't want to cause any problems to you"

Mark refused and said "we want you to live with us, we all will live together, you don't have a family and you will live alone, I urge you, kid Please live here with us".

Maria said:"He is like your father do what he told you to". Sophia said: "Well, I will stay here, but I will pay you a rent". Mark said:" stay here, pay if you want, and if you don't have money don't pay, but don't leave us don't let me get worried about you".

Sophia shook her head and said: Ok

The next day Sofia went to buy her some clothes in order to meet Victor

At the time of the afternoon she was waiting for him and he came on his horse galloping with Guards

Then he got off his horse's back

He asked her: Hello sweetie how is your day?

She said everything is okay

He told her: Have you found a house to buy?

She said: "not yet I live with a nice family, they didn't want me to leave them"

Victor was uncomfortable somewhat and it seems to concern

She said to him: What's wrong?

He said: Do you want to marry me?

She said: yes but your mother will not agree

He told her why don't we elope and get married or we take a house and live in it?

She told him: where to escape you see thieves and bandits are out and here your mother will not leave us alone, she will kill me

Go and persuade her, she is your mother, I envy you that you have got a mother" Sophia cried a little.

He was at the pose of standing, nervous he was thinking and absent-minded, he said:" we have to find a solution"

He told her:" Listen to me, don't leave the place but show me where you live and I'll find a solution" and he said:" I promise you that I will not let you down".

He went with her to see her house and she said: " This is the house where I live but don't come near .I don't want anyone to know that we meet and he saw the house from a far distance.

He got up his horse's back and went quickly to the palace, entered and saw his mother.

There arose a heated discussion between the prince and his mother the Queen

Victor: I plead you my mother I want to marry her and I will not marry any other one, even if it comes to running away with her.

Queen: Victor I have told you my opinion, the girl is poor, she does not have a family, does not have the pedigree, have you got mad?

Victor: " O mother Please, mother I plead you, I beg you "he knelt at her feet and said "I want her, I plead you"

Queen stood up:" Are you mad I have ordered you to close this issue I don't want to hear this from you again"

Victor: "Then don't blame me if I behaved against your will"

The Queen slapped him on face.

He looked at her, and his eyes were drowning with tears

He rushed out of the hall and he was crying

He went on hunger strike and stayed locked in his room away from his mother and father for three days with neither food nor water, and after the three days his mother was knocking the door but he didn't answer.

Guards broke the door and found him unconscious, they called his mother, and she was crying, she said:" summon the doctor", they summoned the doctor

The doctor came and examined him and told them that he needed some care and food.

He opened his eyes while his mother was holding his hands and crying

Mother" he said. "

Tessa answered:, Rest son, don't speak, I beg you don't do such thing to yourself again my son, and cried She told him "Do what pleases you and marry her but don't kill yourself, my son".

He held her hand and kissed it and weeps and told her:" Oh, I love you mom".

When his health improved, he got out of bed and put on his clothes and went to meet Sophia

He knocked at the door, Maria opened and he asked her:" where is Sophia?"

She asked him to wait for a few minutes.

Sophia came out; he held her hands and said:" There is something very important I want you to know, something bad".

He held her hands and they went far.

She said:" well what is it?"

He kept silent and he pretended he was concerned

She was waiting for bad news but he suddenly held her hand and cried and told her:" My mother has agreed upon our marriage.

She smiled and wondered:"really?"

He shook his head: "Yes she did".

"Mom wants to meet you tomorrow to set a the wedding date, come with me to the palace where we will live together"

Sophia said: "No, not now I want to farewell those who have hosted me this day".

The prince: "Well I am waiting for you tomorrow My Princess"

Sophia talked to Mark's family: "This is my last day here and will go to the Palace with Prince Victor.

Mark put his hand on her shoulder and said: "I will miss you my daughter"

Sofia Said" and I will miss you too and mostly your daughter Jasmine, I have liked her so much" Sophia embraced the small girl.

Maria said, I hope to see you soon

Mark said: Yes, the house is open for you all the time, whenever you like to come and visit us.

Sophia said:" I will never forget your support to me; she took 200 gold pieces and put them on the food table.

Mark said: No, my daughter, I have enough money, keep them with you, perhaps you will need them.

Sophia said: "Thank God I have enough money and will send you an amount of money every now and then".

Mark laughed and said: "200 gold pieces, are enough for us to live a year".

Sophia said: I want my family to live like rich people.

Mark said" God bless you and your marriage"

Sophia said: 'thank you, I have to sleep now to get ready to leave and go to the palace.

She packed her staff, farewell them, called the little girl and said to her: "My little kid I will miss you", she embraced her strongly

Victor came along with some of the Guards

He said:" Good morning, My Princess"

She smiled and said: good morning

He said: "Is My Princess ready to leave?"

She said:" Yes"

Let's proceed to the palace to our wedlock

She mounted the horse and rode with him until the entry of the palace.

And he went to the throne hall, Sophia entered, he said timidly Mother, Sophia has come" "

Queen Tessa said:" leave us alone, Victor"

Victor said:" with due obedience, your majesty "He was happy and joyous".

Queen stood up and roamed in the hall and Sophia was watching her.

Sophia said:" I am sorry, your Majesty. I did what you wanted and left and he came back and told me that you approved our marriage"

Queen:" I am very embarrassed concerning high-class people, what am I going to tell them? My son has married a poor girl?" and she began to cry. Then she stood up and said: I will face the matter, engagement will be announced tomorrow, so get ready we will go to the temple to decree your engagement and your name as "princess".

Sophia said:" With due obedience your majesty" she gave the rest of the money to the queen said: "This is the rest of the money I couldn't keep my promise"

Queen said:" No take them in order that people may not say that my son has married a poor girl, but no, she is rich and she has money".

Sophia looked at her and said:"Thank you, your majesty I will go and get prepared for the ceremony tomorrow

Queen Tessa Called servants, and asked 5 maids to go with Sophia to see her room, she entered her room, almost shedding tears of joy and was watching her room and one of her maids said "Your majesty, the bath is ready' she entered, the bathroom was full of candles and warm water in a bathtub full of flowers, she took off her clothes and went down to the water and smelt the roses in the water and the maids cleaned up her body till she ended

Victor knocked at the door, she allowed him to enter.

"My Princess" He said "I missed you", he kissed her hand and said "How is everything?"

She said:"Fine" she was happy and her face was radiating with joy.

Are you ready for the big ceremony tomorrow?"

Yes, I'm ready my prince" she said. "

He sat on the bed and said: 'Well, tomorrow I will sleep next to you after the announcement of our engagement and our wedding officially".

She laughed and was shy.

Victor laughed and said:" I'm also going to take a bath preparing for the wedding tomorrow"

"Good night My Princess" he said.

Good night My Prince "she replied. "

At morning she woke up on the sound of the room door

Who" Said Sophia? "

She said:" I'm the maid", the Queen has sent me to prepare you".

She rose and told her: "Come in"

The maids entered and they started to decorate her hair and clothes, when they finished she seemed like the moon, radiating of beauty like her mother

She went down to the hall and Victor was ready, He entered too and said "what am I seeing?" He was impressed by her gorgeousness and went with haste and kissed her hand and said:" My Princess How beautiful you are today"

She said "thank you too" and her cheeks were red out of shyness

Queen said" people are waiting out",

The Prince and Princess went out and got in the cart, the whole empire were celebrating the marriage of son of the Queen and the people come out waiting for the carriage, all people were in rows, along with roses to spread on them.

The ceremony started Guard came out and after them, prince and princess and people were cheering them God bless your marriage and throwing roses on them and Victor was waving his hand to the people and also the Princess Sofia

They watched on the road to the temple (Fred) he was very drunk, he sat, surprised when he saw the Princess and said" I've already seen her before".

The person next to him asked:" Do you know the princess?" "No how could I know?"

In his hand was a glass of wine, he said maybe she is or perhaps

And walked to his home after watching the parade of the Princess and Prince wedding

Stop suddenly and sat thinking:" By God, I swear, I have seen her somewhere before, in a bar? In ....

He was swinging of wine

He went home and sat down to drink and the image of the girl is still in his head.

He was drunk and wondered where did he saw her

And came out of his room in order to buy some food and he had only two silver pieces, he had some money given by Queen when he led them to the spaceship but he lost this prize in women, drinking and eating. He has become poor now

He wants someone to sell him a piece of bread by his 2 silver pieces, he stopped at the bakery and the empire were talking about the marriage of Princess and Prince, some making jokes on the Prince and Princess. One of them said" I heard that they will be living in the pile of iron, evil bearer (e. g. Spaceship) and sat laughing.

He remembered the girl and the fortified pile of iron, he cried and said:" It is her, it is the girl"

He hugged the man who said the joke and kissed him in his mouth and the man said to him:"go away you drunk"

He said:" I will be rich again I beg you show me where the Queen lives" He continued I mean where are they now? (He was very drunk and couldn't speak well)

He said:"They are in the temple now"

Thanks" said Fred and tried to kiss the man once again"

The man said "where are you going?"

"I will go to see the Queen in the temple ", he said: "They will kill you", he laughed.

He said:" what a screwed man, he will die".

He went to the temple and it was full of Guards

Said the guard:" hey you go away from here"

Fred" I want to meet the Queen   Queen....., he was silent as if remembering her name

The guard said:" Walk away from here, even if you knew the name of the Queen I will not allow you to enter"

Fred:" Please, I want to meet the Princess I don't mean the Princess, the Queen I'd like to talk with her in an important thing"

The guard got out the sword and told him:"go away from here go to your bar go drink, I don't want to kill anyone in the wedding day of the Prince.

Fred Said "well, well, he returned to the house and slept all the day as a result of the severity of the drink.

The prince and princess were on one bed and Prince was flirting with Princess, she made love to him it was the first time in her life

At the morning, he awaked before Princess was teasing her when she was asleep and tickling her, he said to her:" wake up; my mother is waiting in the hall.

Sophia said: " let me sleep some more time, you didn't let me sleep well yesterday I am very tired

"Well "he said I will go and meet my mother and tell her you are tired", he kissed her head and went down

Queen Tessa:" How was your wedding night? Was everything okay?"

Prince Victor said: "Yes mom, we have not slept all night, I am glad my mother" and he embraced his mother.

The Queen said: Do you think I don't rejoice for you? I swear by God I didn't sleep yesterday and I cried and I prayed for you I was worried a little bit, because you will just be a little far from me

Victor said "No, mom you are a crown over my head it is impossible to be far from you, he embraced her strongly, told her:" On earth where would I find such tenderness and warmth of my mother?

She touched his cheeks and told him "I didn't know tenderness and mercy, but when I gave birth to you"

The Queen stood, kissed his head and hugged him.

Fred woke up, he felt a headache and was very thirsty, he drunk water but he didn't find anything to eat, he sat on the bed, he was wondering what happened last night, he doesn't remember anything, he couldn't find but crusty bread and began to soften the bread with water and eat it, he brought his drink and sat drinking

He came out, perhaps to find anyone who sells him food for 2 silver coins, he found only an owner of grocery who sold him 5 apples for 2 silver coins

He knew that his death is near, no money, no food no drink. He returned to the house and was sad, he decided to leave to look for work or someone give him some money

He walked and on his way the man who told the joke saw him and said to him, O are you still alive you drunk man and he laughed.

Fred was surprised what this person says

Fred said to him," what do you mean?"

The man laughed and told him:" It is a natural to say' what you mean' to me yesterday, you were so screwed and drunk

The man continued walking and Fred followed him and said:"what happened yesterday, because I cannot remember anything

We were talking at the bakery and suddenly you screamed and said that you will become rich and you hugged me and kissed me in mouth:"It does not matter, I know you were so drunk" and he laughed

And you said that you will go to meet the Queen

I'm glad you didn't die there

The man went

And Fred sat and tried to remember the incident but he couldn't and he has a headache, he returned home

Fred Sat down and tried to remember the situation. It was like a dream he couldn't remember but one thing; the guard when he took out his sword to his face, but He went back to sleep as he was very tired

The princess and the prince lived the happiest moments of their lives but Sophia didn't forget the coming people of Andre

And was thinking of a way to tell her husband Victor about it, she was hesitated; they were sitting on the bed

she said to him," darling I want to tell you a secret"

Victor felt concern and said:" what is it?"

Will you promise me to keep the secret between us?

"Yes you are my wife" said Victor and I should save your secret

She said:"It is large burden on my shoulders" and she sat crying

He said: Don't make me cry with you, what happened, what is the matter with you darling?"

She said:" I am very scared and cried out of her highest voice

Victor felt worry and anxious but he hugged her and tried to relieve her stress. She cried and finally she became calm.

Victor said: "tell me, what is the matter with you?"

She told him "I am very scared of something I can't face it alone, do you promise me to be with me"

Said Victor:" Yes, I promise and swear to you to keep the secret and to help you"

She asked him" Do you really love me?"

Victor said:" I was going kill myself for you, you needn't ask that question'

She said:"Then I will tell you what I saw and I will not tell you what I didn't and only God knows about my honesty"

She sat down and told him a story like fantasy and he was astonished.

She said:" I opened my eyes to the world finding a sick father his name was Andre , he couldn't sleep at night he saw nightmares and I helped him and was next to him, so I lived all my life like this" he was working a lot and we live in...' Then she stopped talking.

He asked her where? ?

She said "in a spaceship"

And what is the spaceship do you mean "evil bearer"

She shook her head and he got near her and said:" Go on what happened after that?"

I don't know where I am, I didn't know but him in this world, all the time he worked on that ship or, as you call it evil bearer"

I grew older and throughout the time he was working to fix that spaceship and suddenly he stopped working and felt despair

And spend all the time teaching me reading, writing and everything

Victor said: "wait a moment," are these books of magic and sorcery"

She said" No they are ordinary books that relate to life, and she said:' an example for this is in the multiplication table

Like me and you how many do we equate" It is easy, two" said him," Multiply 10 by 1000?" How much?" said she

He sat down to think she said:" very easy 10,000 thousands add zero for the thousand"

He said:" how have you calculated it so fast?" She said," it is science that we need" and she said I have 500 books and I memorize it

Victor said: "Go on, tell me what happened later?"

She asked him "where are we" He told her:" your teaching"

"Yes", she said "one day he was teaching me a lesson on the mother and he was explaining how the tenderness of the mother to her children is"

I cried when I remembered my mother and I told him I want my mother, Andre to me," you know that your mother is dead but it is time to know the truth and see her, and he told me that the next day we will go to see mother and also go to the hill's valley to bring something, I told him: "Well," and I went with him and he said: "that is your mother" and I went to her grave and then I cried and saw another grave next to hers, I asked him about this person ,he hesitated but after a while he told me that he is my father I didn't believe what I had heard I told him:" impossible and you?"

He shook his head:"No" .It was a strong shock to me.

I sat next to their graves for days and he was trying to get near me and I push him away and he sat in front of me telling me that he saved my life and my mother's life and told me how my father died, I asked:" and how did my mother die?"

He told me the death of your mother is mysterious and you are too young to understand such things

I told him do you think that I am a dumb that I cannot understand? He said:"no, I will tell you everything, but you should go with me I will find a way to explain to you the death of your mother"

We went, and on our way, he refused to tell me how my mother died and said that he want some time

We arrived at the Hill's valley, she said:" We saw that the people were all dead and he carried me on his shoulders and said to me,' Close your eyes and we went looking for something".

Victor said, and what is the thing?

She told him it is battery based on power generation in order to operate the spaceship or "evil bearer"

"Oh, Go on" said Victor

Then she said," and we entered a house where we saw an old woman crying and said:" I beg you, don't kill me" she was scared

I went to embrace her and she was crying, he asked her:' is there anyone else living here? She said: 'No" " who did that to the village?"

And the old woman said:" the King's army attacked us at night and kills all people old and young even children"

I went to the well of water and I got down it and I heard the guards who are investigating some people and were looking for someone named Andre

Victor said:" Andre is your non real father"

She said:" yes"

Someone said:' we don't know where he is after he killed his lover and took her crops and the small girl too"

And I was shocked when I heard this and asked her:" do you know her name or the little girl?"

I don't know the name of the small girl, but her mother is called Jesse

I screamed and started crying and he was trying to explain to me what happened to my mother and I shouted on his face, and the old woman embraced me.

Days passed and we returned to the spaceship, I went to my room I was tired of traveling and I didn't sleep well I slept on crying and woke up crying.

Having slept suddenly the ship worked and lights goes on of it even my room became illuminated

He was screaming:"I did it I did it"

And went out of my bedroom and he approached me:" my daughter" he said to me" I did it" and I told him" go away from me I'm not your daughter"

At night when he was sleeping I went close to his room and took the gun

What is the gun?" Victor asked"

She replied that it was a machine made by them and that it kills humans, animals and everything else.

"My mother told me about it when I was young she said that it was a magic stick" he said.

Sophia:" it is not as you think; they have made it, we can make a machine like it if there are available materials"

"That's right" he said "why don't we start that now?"

Sophia: "but we need time until we find the material Andre need a clever blacksmith"

He told her that he will take on this; "go on" he said.

Sophia continued: "I went to his room where he was sleeping, sweetening and speaking to himself as usual. He woke up, his hands were tied in order not to wake up and kill himself, and he looked

At me; he thought he was dreaming

"Sophia, baby" said Andre "what are you doing? Please don't kill me today" but I said:" you killed my mother", he was crying saying:" I beg you, don't kill me today, do it tomorrow"

I told him that I am not stupid to let his people come to our land after they have destroyed their land

He knew it is the day of his destiny, he said:" then do it now but please, bury me next to your mother"

I told him that he didn't deserve that, instead he deserved to be crucified.

And I shot him until he died

I crucified him for two weeks to revenge my mother but Emilia asked me to bury him saying that he has received his punish then I buried him next to the spaceship and I lived with Emilia in the spaceship .one day, Emilia and I were sleeping when we heard the voice of some persons trying to open the door of the spaceship, we woke up afraid; I was shuddering and she was praying. In the morning, I went out of the spaceship ' it was safe, I took what we needed and ran away with Emilia to the pyramid shaped mountain. After a period of time I missed my mom and dad so I went to visit their tombs watching from a distant place to find out that the spaceship had disappeared .I went to my parents' grave and while I was sitting there, I saw the rocket coming up suddenly to the sky. I screamed and said: 'No, Andree's people is coming'"

Victor said: Do you mean the thing that was launched to the sky is a call for them?"

She said:" yes and it is a machine that tells them that there is a new life here now they are coming to occupy our land and take the wealth ".

Victor was impressed; he said:" these words are very serious, you mean that we will die"

She cried saying:" Yes"

He asked her to continue talking

Sophia: " I was afraid, I came back quickly to tell Emilia what happened but she was dead" she stopped a moment crying, before she continue talking :" I buried her and stayed alone, I was so lonely that I was annoyed very much "

"I decided to go to the empire. I slept in a barn until the owner of the house where I live saw me; he said:"come and live with us"

Victor was confused; he said:"what will we do?" Sophia cried and saying:" I don't know. I told you in order to help me"

Victor asked her:" where is the magic stick? Or 'gun' as you call it"

She replied" I threw it in the sea in order to not to be taken ",

Victor said angrily:" Why have you done so?"

Victor said:" Can we make like it?"

Sophia said: "yes we can but it requires some time"

Victor said "how much time we need and how much time they need to come to here?"

Sophia said:" I don't know but Andre told me that he took about 30 years to come to our land"

Victor said:" well, we have enough time but I wish if I was able to tell my mother, she can help us"

She said:"No, please, your mother will kill me"

He said:" Don't be afraid it is our secret and we will try to face them"

 Let's go to bed and think about it tomorrow"

Sophia held his hand and said:" Are you angry with me?"

Victor Said:" No, I would be angry with you in case that you didn't tell me that serious matter"

They slept and she was relieved after she told victor her secret.

Early in the morning she got up and she was vomiting, Victor woke up:"Are you okay?" he asked "yes" Sophia replied "but my stomach hurts me"

He went to his mother's room quickly while she was sleeping

"Mother, mother" she came out of her room and said: "what is the matter?"

"Sophia is vomiting she said that her stomach hurts her"

The Queen laughed and said:"Congratulations, your wife is pregnant and you will become a father and I'm going to become grandmother"

Victor hugged his mother saying: "Are you sure, mother!"

He came back to Sophia and told her that his mother said that Sophia is pregnant and he embraced her saying that he would become a father

I am glad but I have to protect this child and protect my people from the coming occupiers".

Sophia asked him to let her see the spaceship' evil bearer'

Victor said:"well" Sophia went with him and saw the place; she showed him her bed and everything else in the spaceship, when they went out they found the queen.

Sophia and Victor were afraid

The Queen looked at them and said: "what are you doing here?"

Victor:" nothing; I was showing Sophia the" evil bearer"; she haven't seen it before"

The Queen asked them to prepare themselves for the party that would be held for Sophia's pregnancy.

Sophia said:" thank you your majesty"

The Queen told them that she didn't like any person to enter the evil bearer even Victor

Victor agreed: "With due obedience, your Majesty"

They became ready for the ceremony but she was worried about that party; she felt that something bad was going to happen, she decided to hide the gun and she didn't find but the spaceship to hide the gun in , there was a safe that was being opened only by a password that she knew as Andre told her how the safe was being opened.

They were at the party and there were crowds of the elite of the society congratulating her. After they finished the ceremony, they entered to have dinner .Suddenly; she left the dinner .The Queen wondered laughing:" why don't you eat? You should feed my grandson"

Sophia said:"I don't know I, cannot eat well"

Queen said:" Just after the first three months of pregnancy your appetite will be better"

Sofia asked for permission to leave the table because she was tired.

Victor held her hand to leave with her but she told him to stay; "Please, stay here, I want to be alone for some time. I will go out in the fresh air"

"Well, if you need anything, just call for me".

She shook her head agreeing and went out quickly to her room, she took the gun , hide it in her clothes and went out from the back door of the palace, where the spaceship existed, she entered it quickly , opened the safe , put the gun and closed it. When she was on her way to get out of the spaceship, Victor entered and she was scared.

Victor asked: "what are you doing here? Are you mad! Do you want my mother to scold you?"

She replied:" nothing; I remember the past days; in this place I spent my childhood here,

He said:"Let's go before my mother see us"

They went to their room where Victor said:" Please, don't do that again; my mother gets angry easily she doesn't want anyone to mess with the evil bearer." He continued: "I want to tell you a secret"

"What is it?" asked Sophia

He said: "when I was a child, I loved to play in the evil bearer and hold the steering wheel and once I pressed on something

And then a loud sound was heard in the ceiling and then something was launched out"

126

She put her hand on her mouth and said: "Are you who launched the rocket?".

He shook his head" yes, I didn't mean what had happened. I was a child then"

Victor sat down crying; he said: "i feel guilty because I who cause the disaster"

Sophia embraced him and said:" it is not you; it is destiny. It's a test for us to show whether we can protect our land"

"Please, my dear", said Victor "Think about a method of manufacturing the gun

Sophia said: "It is not as easy as you think, May somebody of our generation succeeds in making it; however I have an idea to defend our land, don't worry.

Victor asked her: "For how long it will be a secret?"

She answered:" I don't know, one day you may become a king, and then you and I will be able to face them, they are 30 years before they reach our land.

Let us enjoy our life now; God may help us and destroy them before they reach here"

"Well" said Victor then they went to bed

After 9 months it was time for Sophia to give birth to her baby. Sophia gave birth to a very beautiful baby boy, he resembled his parents. The Queen rejoiced and decided to do a grand ceremony befitting the newborn baby and the great surprise that she will announce in the great ceremony.

There was a declaration about a great ceremony in the empire in which there will be free food and drink.

All people attended the ceremony in the Palace Square to celebrate this great day; the Queen, the Prince, the princess, and the first child went out from the balcony greeting people who were clapping .

The Queen welcomed people then she said: "I am gathering you today to celebrate the first child of Prince Victor, besides; I have appointed him a viceroy ". Victor was surprised; he hugged her saying:" mother!" before she made him wear the crown.

The Queen's decision to appoint her son as a viceroy made Roy; the minister of the Empire, very angry; he believed that he was more suitable for that position and he went out of the ceremony angrily.

Andre stood up and said:" I thank you for coming, I am very happy because: firstly; I have become a father not the father of my son only, but the father of everyone"; people clapped, and he continued:" secondly; I became viceroy, May God help me to manage the affairs of the Empire. I will call my son Alekhandro" Sophia looked at him crying; she hugged him, he kissed her in front of everyone and people were shouting long live Alekhandro, long live Alekhandro.

He said:"It's your turn", she said:" what do I say?"

He told her that she should say anything even if two words to thank them for coming

He asked her to give him the baby to say a word; she was wiping her tears, she said:" thank you for coming today. May God support my husband; Prince Victor thanks you".

Fred was in attendance, he was eating much and didn't care about the ceremony, he became so poor that he didn't find enough food.

When he was eating he saw the girl speaking and began to remember:"I remember this girl; I remember her wedding party; she is the owner of the fortified iron pile", He continued remembering: " I remembered the guard who tried to kill me in front of the temple;

What should I do now?"

He tried to precede more and more in order to meet the Queen but he couldn't because of the large crowd of people

As he approached, they entered the palace.

He asked one of the guards there:" can I meet the Queen?"

The guard said:" Do you think it is a good time for the Queen to meet someone like you?" Fred

Said:" Please, help me; I want to tell the Queen an important issue" The guard said:" Come tomorrow, you will find the minister, the husband of the Queen; you can speak to him"

"Well" he said and went singing;" I will become rich; I will buy clothes and wine , sleep with women and get drunk until morning".

Fred went to his house happily and said:" What will happen if she was not the same girl?"

He said:" No, no... I am sure it is her".

He was hesitant and wanted to see her closely to become sure.

In the morning there was a loud argument between Roy and the Queen..." Why my son did became a viceroy while I am still a minister?!"

The Queen said:" why are you angry isn't he your son?" He said:" he is my son but I deserve that more than him"

The Queen said: "I am the Queen and I am the best to take the right decisions; He already became a viceroy; it's all over"

Roy went to his office angrily.

Fred went to the palace and asked for the Queen or the minister for a serious matter; the guard asked him to wait till he tells the minister who permitted him to enter;

Fred:" O Your majesty, do you remember me?"

Roy:" No, but I think I saw you before"

Fred: I'm the person who showed you the place of the iron pile and the girl.

The minister:" Yes, I remembered you, what do you want?"

Fred:" I know the place of the girl"

The minister:" where is the girl?"

Fred said: "Here in the palace"

The minister:"Speak clearly and briefly"

Fred:" the girl is the wife of Prince Victor"

The minister was angry and said:" Are you crazy or drunk?"

Fred:"I swear, My Your majesty" The minister: "that is a serious talk that may cost you your life"

Fred:"I know that, I just want to see her closely"

130

The minister said:" mm.. That means that you are not sure, you want to leave without your head"

Fred: No, Your majesty; just to be sure so as not to oppress the girl; just one close look"

The minister thought deeply then he said: "well I will invite you to have lunch with us, don't speak very much, try to identify her and shake your head with yes or no, wait here; I will bring some suitable clothes for you"

The minister brought some of his clothes and went quickly to Fred; he locked the door and ordered him to change his ragged clothes."If the Queen asked you about our relation tell her that we're friends and that we didn't have met for a long time and I will tell her that a friend of mine will have lunch with us" said the Minster, "Wait for me here and don't move or make any noise till I come".

Roy went to his son's room and knocked at the door which Victor opened; he told Victor that an old friend of Roy who hadn't been met for a long time will have lunch with them and that he expected Victor and Sophia to greet him if Sophia didn't want to have lunch.

Victor said:" with due obedience, Father"

Victor entered their room where Sophia was playing with her son, he said:"My father said that there is an old friend of him will have lunch with us and he wanted us to be there".

Sophia said:"No, you can go alone, I'm tired"

He said:" No, my father said that we must go together, he also said that if you don't want to have lunch you can go and greet him then leave" "

She said:" Well, I will go for lunch. Take care of our baby till I change my clothes"

Sophia put on her best clothes then they went down where the Queen was waiting for them with Roy and Fred.

Sophia greeted Fred and sat down to the dining table and so did Victor, Fred was starring at Sophia and then looked at Roy shaking his head with yes.

Roy left the dining room so the queen asked:" Why don't you eat?" he said:"I am full" and winked to Fred

Fred stood up saying:" thank you for hosting me".

The Queen was wondering about the matter.

They went to the room where Fred said:" sir; I am hungry, I didn't finish my lunch yet"

Fred gave him 200 gold pieces warning him:"Don't tell anyone otherwise I will cut your head and be no longer here again'

Fred took the money, he was very happy: "thank you your majesty, it will be a secret" then he left.

Roy sat down thinking about what he would do if Fred was lying, and why would he lie as he was the only person who saw her.

He stayed two days on this status and the queen asked:" what is the matter with you? "He tells her was exhausted because of work.

Finally, he decided to ask Sophia some questions.

He said:"Dear Sophia, what about coming to walk with me"

"Ok. Your majesty" she said, they walked out of the palace...

He asked her about her father and how her childhood was, she was amazed at his question, he said to her:"Excuse me I want to know everything about your past life". She sat talking to him.

When they passed by the spaceship, Roy said:" Look! Have you ever seen it before?" She said: "Yes, my husband Victor showed it to me"

"let's get in and talk a little; I didn't enter it a long time ago" said Roy

She said:" No, Your majesty; the queen warned about entering there" but he said:"Don't worry, I'll be with you, she always feels afraid of everything, let's enter"

They get in the spaceship; they were watching and Roy was astonished, he said to Sophia:"Look! Do you think it is a creation of God?"

She said: "Perhaps, but I don't think so"

When they passed by the cockpit, Roy said:" Look! What is this thing" her tongue slipped saying:"It's the control room"

He suffocated her saying:" How did you know that its name? "She said that Victor told her.

He said: "I know who you are and that you lived here, I know everything about you but I want to know where the magic stick is"

She wondered:" what stick? I don't know what you are talking about"

He said:"Then, I will tell the Queen that you are the girl she is looking for ".

You must give me the magic stick within 3 days otherwise, I'll tell the Queen about everything. He moved his hands off her and went out.

She fell to the ground and began to cry looking to the sky:"mom, dad, help me"

She came out of the spaceship and went to the palace crying; she wiped her tears before she enter the palace so as not to be noticed.

She entered the hall where Tessa; the Queen, Roy; the minister and her husband Victor were drinking tea.

Victor stood up saying:" Sophia, come and have tea with us ", but She said;" No, thank you, I am tired and I want to feed my baby"

Roy called her:"Sophia"

Sophia stood and said:" with due obedience, your majesty"

He said:" I want to talk with you a little"

Sophia returned: "With due obedience, your majesty"

She sat down listening to Roy who said:" What's the child's news today?

"He is fine" She said

Roy said:" Victor, what is the name of the place in the evil bearer where you found a chair and you liked to play in.

Victor laughing:"How could I know?"

Roy:" I remember that you told me its name as control or something like that"

Victor: "maybe; I don't know its name"

Sophia left the place saying:"I am tired", then she went to her room and began to cry

Victor entered:" My Princess, Oh My Princess" he said.

She wiped her tears when he sat down beside her saying: "What is the wrong with you?"

"Are you okay dear?""

Sophia: "Yes I am fine"

Victor:" Where is Alekhandro?"

Sophia: "he is sleeping"

She was trembling; he held her hand and looked to her saying: "Are you fine, baby"

He touched her head:" What is the matter with you?"

Sophia:" Nothing, just I'm tired"

Victor:" Do I call the doctor?"

Sophia:" No, I want to take some rest"

They went to bed, however she didn't sleep. , she was thinking what to do; she thought to escape but it was a bad idea as she couldn't leave her son. She also thought to give the gun to Roy and as a result her secret would be revealed and her husband would be angry of her because she didn't tell him where she hid the gun.

She had to choose one of 4 options, giving the gun the Roy, killing Roy, escaping, or staying in the palace waiting for Queen's word.

Finally, she decided to kill him in order to save her secret for eve. She thought that if the murder was revealed, she would escape; she had a gun to protect herself.

In the morning she got up and went down, the Queen was sitting on the throne and her husband beside her; they were having coffee.

She said:"good morning, Your Majesty"

They replied: "good morning"

Roy and Sophia looked at each other then Sophia winked to him; she left the place and Roy followed her.

At the door she said:" Meet me at the evil bearer, I will give you the magic stick"

He said:" It is the right decision .Well, when?"

Sophia:" Tonight, beware of being seen by the Queen or my husband"

Roy:" Well, don't worry".

The Queen entered and said to them:" Is there a secret?"

Roy said laughing:" No, she tells me about the bad behavior of Victor; she says he is sometimes nervous and I told her to be patient, is it true Sofia?"

Sophia:" True, Your majesty"

Queen:" Well, let me talk to him in this matter"

Roy:" No she has delegated me for the task and I'm going to talk to him"

With sunset she went to the spaceship and took out the gun. An idea came to her mind.

Roy entered asking for the magic stick.

She said:" I want you to swear to God not to hurt me and keep our secret. All my life, I didn't do what to be punished for; I am a victim and the offender is dead".

He swore saying:" I Never, I wouldn't think to hurt you; you are like my daughter you are my son's wife and your baby is my grandson, come on, give me the magic stick".

She took the gun out of her pocket and gave it to Roy. He asked her to tell him quickly how it works. She said:" I don't know, try pressing on this thing (meaning the trigger) and it will kill"

He stood and put the gun to her head saying: "Thank you" and pressed the trigger but it didn't work .He caught her hair and slapped her saying:"Are you fooling me you, treacherous, he beat her and said:" tell me how it works, tell me",

"I don't know" said Sophia "Wait I have remembered; you should read the magic books so as it may work. Andre did so.

He was sitting for days reading then magic started working".

Roy: "Where are the books?"

Sophia:" They were in Pyramid shaped mountain. I hid them"

"Listen to me, tomorrow or the day after tomorrow, go and bring me the books and do no tell anyone otherwise I will kill you..."

Suddenly, Victor entered; he was shocked by the seen

Sophia was on the ground and his father was pulling her hair.

137

Victor:" Father, what are you doing, what happened to you? Leave her", then he caught Sophia saying: "What are you doing here?"

Roy came out saying:" I have warned her not to enter here, but she disobeyed me and the queen. I saw her messing around here"

Roy planned to kill Sophia, snatch the gun and tell the Queen that Sophia is the girl who lived in the spaceship but his plan failed.

Victor shouted:" How many times I told you not to come here have you forgotten what my mother said? Do you want to make troubles for us! Go out, if I see you here, I will punish you"

He pushed her from behind so she fell to the ground and her leg was wounded.

Victor continued: "Leave before my mother sees you"

She went to her room and sat crying, she lifted her dress to find her legs were all bloody

She said:" what have I done to be punished? Why people punish me for things I didn't do? Why, oh why?!"

Victor entered and saw the blood, he was worried about her, he went running around asking for help and asked for the doctor

The doctor came and put some sterile on the wound and wrapped it.

The Queen entered and said:" What happened?" Victor said "We were racing but she fell to the ground"

The Queen sat beside her and said: "Thanks to God for your safety, my daughter"

Roy entered pretending compassion and tenderness:" My daughter, I heard of what happened to you" "he kissed her head:" Are you Ok.

Now?"She said:" I'm fine. Please, I want to take some rest. I am tired".

"Well" he said" Let's go out"

They went out and she sat crying for two days, she didn't eat anything, she wished she was dead.

She didn't speak to anyone and hadn't met any person.

Roy went to her to tell her that her illness will not help her. He also told her not to pretend the disease. "Tomorrow we will go" said Roy

Sophia:"How could I go with you? You promised not to hurt me but you tried killing me"

Roy:" I haven't tried killing you. I was just trying the gun to see whether you are honest"

Sophia: "and what makes me sure if we go there you will not kill me".

Roy: "I promise you" he said, I want the books"

:" Suppose I agreed to go with you; how will you convince the Queen and my husband that we will go together, they will not let us do; Victor and the Queen will go with us and our plan will be revealed".

Roy:" You are right, I will make a plan for this; you have escaped from me this time, but I will find a solution soon"

He met Victor at the room door when he was going out.

Victor:" father, what are you doing here?"

Roy:" I wanted to see the baby and apologized to her for what had happened"

Victor entered the room and said to her, *"you haven't eaten anything for two days, what is the matter with you? Tell me, I'm your husband and protector, I promise to keep your secrets"*

Sophia:*"Nothing, believe me"*

Roy: *"Then come with me to have lunch, or you would be hiding something".*

Sophia said: *"Well I, I will go down with you for lunch"*

Sophia went with Victor for lunch. When Roy saw her he said: *"I am delighted that you are well; he hugged her whispered:"If the plan failed today, we will escape tomorrow" They*

Sat down for lunch then Roy said:*" Sophia, I see you are fine what about going to ramble outside the Empire and hunt some animals tomorrow"*

Victor said:*" Good idea; what is your opinion, Mother?*

The Queen said:*" No, who manages this country! You can go without me"*

Roy said:*" No, my son, stay here to take care of the child"*

The Queen said: *"Don't not worry about the child, I Will take care of him, go with them tomorrow"*

Sophia stood up and went to her room.

Sophia was crying when she said: *"What do I do dad, mom save me please, I am very tired what do I do, could I escape and leave my baby; and then my secret will be revealed"*

Or could I escape with Roy?! He would probably kill me"

140

Victor entered and asked Sophia about her opinion about his father's idea

She replied:" I don't know"

While she was thinking, an idea came to her mind.

She came out of the room and went to the minister Roy and said:"Your majesty, tomorrow I will go with you"

Roy was very happy

She said:"I will show you the place of the books and return back"

Roy: "well, well" said he: "At dawn, when they are sleeping, I will go out with you"

She couldn't sleep all night, she was hugging the baby and crying:"If I die, you have a father and family who can protect you" she said that then she hugged him crying and saying:"It may be the last time to see you ".

She breastfeed her child in order not to cry and quietly she left her bed in order not to be heard by Victor

She put on her clothes and went out where she found Roy waiting, he said:" Quickly. Why are you late?"

She went out of the palace and rode a carriage then they left. The Queen saw them from the window, she came down quickly and asked the guards where they went, one guard told her that the minister said, he went hunting"

The Queen asked: "Is Victor with them?" but the guard said:" No"

The Queen was amazed.

She went to the top and awoke Victor saying:"Your father and your spouse have gone, they left you"

Victor rose up amazing:"Where have they gone?"

The Queen:" One of the guards said they're going to hunt"

Victor:" Well, I will try to catch up with them"

Victor went out looking for them but he didn't find them in the places of hunting and he returned

He said to the Queen:" I didn't find them"

Queen Tessa:" I am worried"

Victor:" Mother, you are always so, you are worried about everything .just a father went with his daughter. Let them enjoy and they will return by sunset"

They arrived the mountain and went up to the cave where Sophia gave him the books

She asked:" Can I go now; my son is hungry and my husband is worried about me"

He said;" No, wait, we have a much time, sit down"

She sat down and he said;"Which book?"

She gave him a book of mathematics .It was too complex

He said: "How does work?"

Sophia:" I swear, I don't know; if I knew, I would own the whole world"

He tied her and said:" Do you think I am stupid. You lived with him since you were young and you know everything", then he beat her.

Roy: "If you want to be released, you have to tell me how the magic works.

I want to own the world by magic".

Sophia: "Well, set me free and let me read to confirm for you".

He removed the tie then she said: "I want to go to the bathroom" and he said: "Quickly, and don't go far " she said:" don't be afraid, I'll be here in the cave".

She went to the rock and took two bullets then she came back to him and said: "let's begin"

Sophia said: "We have to cover the magic stick". Roy brought his garment and covered the gun then she sat reading the equations for an hour and a half then she entered the bullet inside the gun and said:" I have finished the first book lets test it, but we have to read all of the books we to work longer"

"Give me the stick" he said," No I will try it in front of you" she replied

He said:" Let's go" They went looking for a goal for haunting; they found a deer; she shot it and it died

He was happy; he took the gun and said:" I want you dead like the deer, my daughter".

He tried to shot it the second shot but it didn't work

She said:"You saw everything you, please, let me go"

He said:" I want to try it myself" She said:" well..."

They returned to the cave, she said:" You have to read all the words written, don't err and cover the magic stick as I did"

She covered the gun with the garments and asked him to read, and then she entered the bullet and sat waiting.

He got tired of reading about 200 pages; he reached half the book and said:"Do you think this is enough?" she said:" No, go on"

He continued reading the book till he finished , then he revealed the garment and caught the gun towards her but she jumped out of her place , he shot her, she was about to die. He laughed saying that it worked.

Sophia:"It works now, let me go to the baby" and she began to cry

Roy:" Let's take all the books"

Sophia:"What if they asked about them, what will you say?"

Roy:" I will tell them that we found them while we were hunting"

Sophia:"You promised to let me live in peace. Please, stay away from me; I want to live with my son and husband"

Roy:"I have promised you, you are now free"

He sat laughing:"I will kill anyone by this magic stick"

Her plan succeeded and she convinced him it is magic

They returned to the empire, and she was afraid as Victor was angry, they entered the palace and Roy ordered the guards to transfer the books

Victor received them at the entrance gate with a laugh:" Why haven't you taken me with you?" His father said:" You were asleep and we didn't want to wake you. Take the deer to the palace in order to be cooked and put the books in my room.

Victor:" What a plenty of books!"

Roy:" We found them while we were hunting".

Victor didn't comment then he went to his room.

After Sophia went to her room Victor asked her: "Are these the books which you told me about?"

She didn't say a word

Victor continued: "Then my father knows"

Sophia wept as she told him:" Your father knows everything about me and he threatened me either I show him the books and the gun or he will kill me or tell your mother".

She continued crying:" What could I do? What could I do? Do you want me to die?"

He sat down on the chair and said:" when I saw you that day in the evil bearer; was he beating you for that reason?"

And he cried out "Why haven't you told me?"

She was crying:" I was afraid .He has threatened me if I tell anyone, he will kill me"

He said: "No I will not let him do that and I will tell my mother to end up everything Things got worse and I must put an end to this".

Victor asked: "Did you found the gun?"

Sophia:" Yes, it is in his possession, but he is unable to use it because he does not have bullets, I convinced him that it was magic. Your father tied me with"

Ropes and tried to kill me twice. He threatened me either the gun works, or he will kill me".

Victor: "Impossible, I don't believe it".

He got out of the room and Sophia followed him:" Please, no more problems. Do you want me to die, he has promised me that he will leave me away and took whatever he wants, and he is unable to do anything with it".

Victor:" and if the magic stick does not work, what will you do? He will come again and tell that you are a liar, beat you, and may kill you I know my father I know that he will not leave you until he gets whatever he wants"

Victor continued: "I will tell my mother about everything and even about people of Andre; everything, she is our Queen and she knows what is good for us.

"

Sophia fell to her knees crying

He went down to his mother and said:" Mother, I want to tell a very serious thing, but I want you to promise me"

The Queen:" Well, what do you want me to promise you?"

Victor: "Do you promise me not to harm my wife and to forgive her"

The Queens:" You always know, I always forgive; I'm not a bad mother"

Victor:" Then promise me now."

The Queen:" I promise you not to hurt your wife and forgive her, but what is the matter? You make me worried"

Victor: "my wife is ... is ...

Sophia entered saying:" ...is the girl who lived in the evil bearer"

Victor turned to her:" Sophia, darling"

Sophia entered and began telling her whole, and even acts of Roy

Queen Tessa:" I cannot believe what I am hearing, it is serious,

Do I put my husband in prison or Jail my son's wife or fight the coming occupiers, what can I do?"

"Guards" She called for the guards who entered immediately,"Come with me" she ordered before she looked to Sophia and said:"It wouldn't go through without punishment, I swear to God"

"Guards, follow me" said the Queen, she was angry, she went to the room of Roy where he was reading a book of physics and wondering what are these symbols and how could he use them

She entered with the guards and said:"Where is the magic stick?"

He asked "What stick are you talking about?" the gun was covered with Roy's garment.

The Queen:" I knew everything. Give me the magic stick or ..."

147

Roy: "Or what? Come on"

The Queen:" You know very well what I can do"

Roy stood up and said:" It's mine, I who found it" and pulled his sword attacking her; he stabbed her then guards killed him.

The Queen fell wounded and bleeding; the guards carried her to her room and brought a doctor

When Victor saw his mother, he said:" what happened" The guards told him that the Minister Roy stabbed the queen.

He asked:" Where is my father?" and they replied:"He died"

Victor was faint and Sofia was crying and trying to awake her husband

They carried him to his room and when he came back to his consciousness; he went quickly to the Queen's room screaming;" Mother, Mother"

The doctor came out of the room and said:" She is seriously wounded" They stitched the wound but she is bleeding. If bleeding does not stop within a few hours she will die, I'm going to bring a medicine for her"

Sophia stood at the door of the Queen's room looking at her husband who was crying for his mother saying:" mother, don't leave me"

She sympathized her husband and the Queen too.

And suddenly Sophia remembered that there are many medicines in the spaceship that in which she may find something that can save the queen's life. She went hurrying to the spaceship, she opened the reservoir, she found many medicines and she kept searching and reading pamphlets and medication instructions. She found an injection medicine to stop bleeding, she took it with the needle and went, speeding, to the queen's bedroom. She stopped at the entrance of the palace and Sophia was talking to herself: "Why shall I save her life and she is danger to me. Perhaps when she recovers, she may kill me or put me in jail.

She hesitated a little, but her kind heart couldn't stop her from doing the good thing. She entered the palace and she went to the queen's bedroom.

She said: to Victor I found a medicine

Victor said: what are you waiting for?

Sophia said: I am afraid that it may harm her and

He asked: "Is there any harm worse than this?" come on, do your best.

She pulled the needle and put it in her vein. And suddenly after minutes the bleeding stopped.

The doctor returned, he brought a medicine for her too and he was fascinated by what he had seen. He said: The bleeding had stopped, thanks to gods

He said: if the bleeding stops till morning, she would live. At morning and the queen is sleeping, she woke up finding Victor and Sophia sitting beside her.

Victor cried my mother and kissed her hands.

The queen said: did you saw what your father did to me, he was about to kill me

Victor said: yes, mother I have seen what happened.

149

The queen said: where is he now?

Victor said: he died in his bedroom.

She said: announce his death and make a funeral, he is your father dear son, then bury him Victor said: well

The queen looked to Sophia and said: and you what do you want from here? All what happened is because of you, get out from my bedroom, I do not want to see you here.

Victor said: Mother, Sophia is the one who saved your life.

The queen said: No, but gods who saved my life, I do not want to see her face.

Sophia went out and her eyes were full of tears, she went to her bedroom.

Victor entered Sophia's bedroom, he hugged her and said: don't worry, my mother always do this ,after she gets well, she will change her way with you.

It is announced in the empire that the queen's husband Roy has died and he was buried, the funeral and receiving condolences was in the palace.

After two months. The queen became in a good health, she ordered to feed all the empire celebrating her recovery.

At dinner time, the queen was sitting on the table head for the first time after her illness. She sat down, Victor kissed her hand and Sophia came to kiss her hand, the queen pulled her hand back and said: don't get near me.

Victor looked at his mother, have you forgotten your promise to me?

She said: I will not forget, but I will not let this pass without punishment, I swear to gods, finish your dinner and follow me to the hall.

Victor said: Mother, do not be hard on her, she is the mother of my children and she is the one who saved your life, I swear to god if she was not here, you might be dead.

She answered: do not stand against your mother to defend her.

Victor left the dinner silently, he was angry.

The queen said: to Sophia follow me to the hall.

The queen sat on the throne and said "choose one of these two punishments either to be imprisoned in a room in this palace and no one see you, you only watch your husband and your son everyday from outside the iron bars or to leave the palace without money or anything and live the rest of your life outside the palace in the empire without your husband nor your son and you are prohibited to meet them except through my permission, and if he sleep with you and you become pregnant and brake my words, you will be dead, I do not want to see you here as long as I am alive, think well and decide".

Sophia said" but what about my son, who will bring him up and take care of him?"

The queen said" your son will be under my care".

Sophia said " with due obedience, your majesty" and went.

Sophia went to her bedroom and sat down. Victor asked her "what did my mother tell you?"

she answered" she gave me two choices :either to live in a room where I will be imprisoned, I will never leave, only I can see you from outside the iron bars or to leave the palace and be free without you. I am confused"

Victor said "no, you will not go and she will not imprison you, wait I will try to persuade her and if she would not be persuaded, I will leave the palace with you"

Sophia said "obey your mother's order and do not act folly, you are the vice queen and one day you will become a king and I will be beside you, don't worry about me, please do not worry I will be ok.

Victor said "choose getting out from the palace and we will meet from time to time, do not be afraid I will try to convince my mother."

Sophia prepared her clothes and stuff, then she went out to say good bye to them and her son.

The queen said" what is in your hands?"

Sophia said" my clothes"

the queen said" I told you get out without anything, only get out with what you are wearing now like the first time where you entered this palace before".

She ordered the servants to inspect her and they did not find anything with her.

She said "now get out and I do not want to see you again, and do not forget your promise or I will..."

Victor said" mother, I beg you, you had promised me to forgive her".

The queen said "do not make me change my judgment".

Victor got angry and said to her "you cannot prevent me from seeing her".

The queen said go meet her, but if you sleep with her, I will make an order to kill her, if you love her and want her to stay alive, stay away from her, I will let you marry who have more wealth, beauty and pedigree. He looked at her and said "No, I will not marry anyone except her, even if I stayed my whole of life alone without a wife". He went out and also Sophia did. Sophia went to her old family's house, Mark and Maria, they welcomed her. Sophia said "I have missed you so much and longed for Jasmine" .Mark said" there is a surprise, my wife, Maria, is pregnant now and we are going to have a new baby" Sophia congratulated Maria and then she sat down and cried a little. Mark asked her" what is wrong with you?" she answered: "the queen expelled me from the palace Mark asked "why?". She said "she has accused me of making problems in the palace". Mark said "this house is yours, if you want, we will get out and sleep in the street and you stay here, we will not forget your kindness with us" Sophia said "thank you all, you are my family and I will help you as much as I can".

A year passed

Her son "AleKhandro" has grown up and became two years old and Victor did not miss anytime without meeting her at the exit door of the empire. Sophia offered him to marry another woman, but Victor refused and said "no other woman will not enter my life, you are my first love and the last ...I only love you" and without consciousness, they exchanged kisses and they went outside the empire and he made love to her. Sophia cried and said "I will die if the queen knew about this, I beg you, do not do it again, you know me, I am weak with you and I cannot resist your love".

Victor said "how could she know that we are here, no one sees us" and he promised her that it will be the last time....but it happened again many times.

Victor said "I cannot live without you, I began to hate being at the palace, it became drear and dark without you and what eases my suffering and pain is our son AleKhandro ".

Sophia said "your mother is very old now and sooner or later she will die and I will return to you".

He said "I cannot stand more, I will try to persuade my mother again, and may her heart be softened. Victor tried to persuade his mother to allow Sophia to come back because Sophia is the only one who can stop the attack.

The queen refused

Victor said" my mother, please understand me, Sophia is the only one who can make the magic sticks works and save us, Victor sat to explain her that" this thing is not made by magic, but it is man-made like us and coming people exceeded us thousands of years by science, this is the secret"

The queen didn't agree with and she said "you are deceived with these words, go and persuade her to teach me magic of the stick in exchange for giving back her husband and her son" Victor got happy.

He went to Sophia to tell her what his mother wants as Sophia may find a way to convince his mother.

Victor went to the family that she lives with. He knocked the door and Maria opened, He said "tell me where is Sophia quickly?" she said "No, I do not know. She took her stuff and left and she left you this message". He opened the message in which Sophia said that she is pregnant ...."I will escape away in order not to be killed by your mother, take care of our son. I love you
Sophia
Victor got angry and he kept searching for her till sunset, he did not

154

find her. he gone mad .his mother asked him" What is wrong with you, my son?"

He replied "nothing, mother "He became nervous. The queen said "did you persuade her to give me the secret of the magic sticks. Victor said "no I have not met her and I do not know where she has gone"

The queen laughed "I have told you that she is crafty and she does not let anyone to know her secret"
a year passed he did not see her, he searched for her everywhere till he despaired and thought that she died. The queen was worried about her son. And in the pyramid shaped mountain while Sophia was giving birth, she cries and cries till she had a beautiful baby; she lived with her daughter alone in a cave. The winter started and snow started to fall and the girl got sick from the cold weather. Sophia was afraid about her daughter, she may die, she decided to sacrifice her life for her daughter and come back to the empire to find a warm place, she entered the empire infiltrating like the first time when she first entered the empire.
She went to Maria's and Mark's house, she knocked the door, Maria opened the door, she cried and said "this is Sophia"

Mark did not believe his eyes, he said "Sophia, where were you? Your husband was searching for you everywhere and gave us money and said "if Sophia came, tell me' who is this baby?"

Sophia said "this is my daughter"

Mark stayed silent and looked at the girl, he thought her an illegal girl. Mark arose from his place, while saying in his heart "perhaps she was hijacked or rapped... what a poor woman?!

Sophia said "wait, sit down, I want to talk with you."

155

Mark sat down and she said " This is the prince Victor's daughter and the queen warned me not to sleep with my husband or become pregnant, she will kill me, so I escaped "She stayed crying then she said "my daughter was about to die from cold so I escaped to come here."

Mark stood and hugged her, he said "thank god that you are ok". He continued "the most important thing is to rest, and do not tell anyone about your place even your husband for he may go to his mother and tell her the truth and she will kill you or torture you...come on, Maria,we should sleep and leave her to rest "they went to sleep and Maria brought some old clothes of her daughter Jasmine, and she gave them to Sophia, she hugged her and said "thank you "

Days and months passed and her daughter became five months old and she was staying home afraid. The clothes became narrow on her daughter and she has been unable to endurance, she decided to go shopping to buy clothes for the girl. While she was doing shopping. Two guards saw her and they bet that if she is the princess Sophia or not. One of them came near to her and greeted her he said "Princess Sophia ,how are you?"

She was terrified and said "Hello". The guard said "I have not seen you since long time and I would like to greet you and who is this baby?".

She said "And what is your business? Are you here to greet me or to ask about the baby" .

The guard said "I am sorry, your majesty, I do not mean this".

He went to the other guard and said "This is her ..She is the princess Sophia but who is the baby with her?.

The other guard said "she may get married".

The guard said "you fool , she is still the Prince Victor's wife".

The other guard said "how is the baby is the prince's son and she lives here not with prince Aleksandro in the palace?!"

The other said "there is a secret, what is your opinion?, we should tell the queen ,she may reward us "

He said "well" . They went to the queen and told her that they saw Princess Sophia holding a baby in her hand.

The queen got angry and said "what ?! A baby?! Had she disobeyed my orders ..Are you sure ?"

They said "yes , we are sure ,but we do not know if the baby is hers or not. "

The queen said "well "and gave everyone of them money and they went.

The queen stayed thinking, she said "she may not be pregnant from Victor "then said "Victor did not see her since long time, I always asked about her news and he said that he did not see her, there is a secret..O guards !....call Victor"

Victor came he said "your order, mother" she said "since when was the last time you saw Sophia "

He said "since a year or more", asked him" have you slept with her?

He stayed silent and then said "no ,why do you ask mother?

She said "tell me the truth and do not be afraid and do not lie, if you say the truth , I will save the young child "

He said "I will, but tell me where did you see her?

157

She said "the guards saw her in the market and she was holding a young baby "

He ran ,hurrying to go for her ,the queen cried and said "answer me "he said "yes mother the child is mine.

She cried loudly and said "you sentenced her to death, this is the penalty of disobeying the queen..O guards, go after him and bring me Sophia immediately and let him take the baby"

The guards caught up with the prince, the prince stood at Mark's house and knocked the door, and Maria opened. He asked "where is Sophia "

She got confused and said "you know that she escaped",

Prince Victor pushed the door and entered, he found Sophia crying and she said "why did you come here? I will die "

He hugged her and said "you will not die, I swear to god, if you died, I would die after you" he hugged the baby girl and said "she looks like you, what did you name her?"she answered" Emilia, I have visited her grave and said that if I give birth and my daughter lived, I will name her after your name "

Suddenly the guards broke into the house, they entered and pulled her from her hair.

Prince Victor said "leave her , I am the prince Victor, I order you to leave her now, they pulled her and two of the guards caught him while he was crying "leave her or I will kill you" Victor took the baby Emilia and caught them up to the palace. The guards entered her to the queen. She was crying "I am sorry, I beg you forgive me " and began to kiss the queen's foot .

The queen said "stay away from me..I will not forgive you ,you have disobeyed my order "she held her hair and said "I do not want anything from you, I ordered you to stay away from my son and to leave him to live his life guards, send her to the prison and do not let anyone enter there even the prince Victor and tomorrow's morning you will kill her in front of people in order to be a lesson to others".

They took her, she was crying "I beg you, I want to bring up my daughter, she is your granddaughter "

The queen said "I will bring her up like I brought up your son, Aleksandaro ,...

Come on" they pulled her while crying ,they took her to prison .

Victor entered "mother, where is Sophia "She said "she is good and she is at my hospitality tonight "

He said "I want to see her"

She said "tomorrow you will see her and take her forever"

He said "please mother, do not make any thing that you will regret "

She cried and said "and what do you like in her? I told you to leave her and I will make you marry a woman who is better than her, but you refused, what do you want me to do for you? She is here to make problems and spoil our relationship, she is liar and crafty ,she knows the magic stick secret, but she does not want to tell anyone about it , my son, I am your mother and I know your advantage"

He said "my advantage is to return my wife back home "

She said "your wife will die in front of people tomorrow morning"

He lost his temper and cried, he said "what is the guilt of this child? Look, at her mother, do you want her to live without a mother "

She said "I will let you marry another one "

He said "I told you that I will not marry any woman except Sophia. And even if she died, I will die with her, I will not live without her, do you understand me ?"

Tears was in the eyes of his mother, she said "this is my last decision

"Victor said " a last request, my mother "

She said "what?" he said "

I want to see her please mother "

she said" O guards ,take him and inspect him before he goes to the prison"

The guards took him and he entered the prison, he hugged Sophia while she was crying "they will kill me tomorrow "

He shock his head ,crying he kissed her hands, her head and everything in her "

Sophia Said "Please, do not let them kill me please, please" and she fell on her knees Victor could not speak,

Sophia asked him "do you promise to do something for me?"

He said "yes, I promise"

She said "take care of my children ,teach them and make them memorize the books that you brought with your father, tell them "if you love your mother ,learn" and make them memorize well "and she went to the pyramid mountain where is there a small cave inside it a rock that is under it a pistol and ammunition about 200 bullets enough to kill Andre's people.

Victor cried "why haven't you told me and where is the pyramid shaped mountain "

She said "I hid it for the coming Andre's people, I did not want to tell anybody because I was afraid to waste the rest of bullets, please, do not give them to anyone even your mother"

He said "where is the mountain ,say quickly"

She described to him the pyramid mountain place and he kissed her and said "I promise ,I will return and save you "and he went out and

She cries "do not give it to your mother, please, please" he went to his mother and said "mother, Sophia wants to keep her life in exchange for working magic sticks ,do you agree?"

The queen stayed thinking, she said "Well, I agree but under a condition, to see the magic sticks working in front of me now"

He said "but the place is very far, I am afraid I might be late" the queen laughed and said "I know that it is an intrigue from her to stop the judgment, she cannot lie to me at this time, but I will give you a lead time. After the sun is out, I will kill her ,you have enough time, we are now in the morning" he rode his horse and went while the queen watching him from the window while he was going, hurrying up on his horse.

It is sunset and the queen is worried about her son. The morning is about to rise and Victor did not appear.

The queen said "if the sun is out ,excite her". Victor was searching for the pyramid mountain till he found it ,he entered the cave and started to search for bullets ,he returned quickly on the horse and he was saying please, sun, do not go out till I return back" and was saying "be late a little"

161

The morning light started to get out while he was hurrying up at full speed.

Slowly the night came out till the sun showed rows of orange he was crying, "O sun ,Stop at your place ,please, his eyes were full of tears on his beloved .he arrived in the empire and get into the gate , but he was too late, he found the people gathering and her head is on the ground

He cried "No, no" he came down from his horse and he moved the people away, he hugged her ,he was crying and shouting "Sophia "and the queen was watching him while he was hugging her , her eyes were full of tears

She said "I am sorry, my son, you are too late".

Victor became sick after her death and he particularly saddened by her, he did not meet his mother since Sophia's death. Once, he dreamt about Sophia as she was saying to him "do you want to come with me to the sky and live with me" he said "Yes, and she held his hands and pulled them up and he was watching clouds while they were going up, they can see the end of the sky, but a flock of goose stopped them ,they hit them and a goose hit Sophia's hand and fall she said "do not forget our promise" he woke up frightened, He went out from his bedroom and went to his father's bedroom and took all the books and started to teach his children, and keep their mother's promise, he began with teaching Aleksandro reading and writing and he was meeting his mother, but not like before he greatly changed. The queen tried to make him marry she made every period a party and invite the most beautiful girls in the city to the palace and send them to him to marry one but he refused and sometimes goes to his room and close on himself

After eight years

His mother became ill and he did not went to see her...all of his time was in his bedroom teaching his children reading and writing and suddenly a guard came ,he told him that his mother died, he cried on parting her and mourning was declared by him and he buried her then he became the king of the empire and his son Aleksandro the vice king

Whereas Emilia likes reading, she memorized all books as her mother requested .Andre's people are coming and King Victor, his children and his people are ready to stop them

20 years passed

Victor became 58 years old ,His son29 years old and Emilia 25 years old victor got married while Emilia does not because she loved to stay alone and read books and she does not like social life,

one day the king Victor was sleeping and there was a voice shacked throughout the empire, the king and Aleksandro were frightened, they went out and saw the space-ship and king Victor shouted "be ready, be ready "and he said to his son Aleksandro "take some soldiers and follow the track of evil barrier quickly.

'

Chapter2

Prince Aleksandaro and some soldiers went after the spaceship, it was very quick and then it disappeared and he heard it's landing sound when it hit the ground. They hurried towards it until they reached it. He ordered the guards to stop at their places and Aleksandaro watched them from afar, their cries of joy were clear while they were celebrating landing. He sent some guards to King Victor to tell him about its landing place. They went hurrying to the empire, they said to the king "prince Aleksandaro said that they have landed and he is there waiting for your orders "king Victor went over his horse and prepared the army. The king said to the army "here, they are, they have come to seize our land, gold and wealth, so fight them till the last solider and destroy them. The army said "long live the king, long live the empire"

His daughter Emilia stopped him and said "no, wait here, they may be armed ".

the army moved towards the ship and Aleksandaro was watching them from afar and waiting for king Victor, and in the morning, they opened the ship door and they landed happily in their first day morning, they were walking and playing around the ship, they were thirty two persons, some of them were born in the spaceship and some died.

Aleksandaro, hiding, he was waiting for his father, the sun went down and lights of the ship turned on and at the midnight, king Victor arrived with the army.

Aleksandaro said "Father, they are inside now, they have closed the door, they go out at morning, to play and when the sun goes down, they go back inside. The king said "well, stay here, I will spy on them from near. ".king Victor went alone and he got closer to the ship, he heard them while they were singing "we have reached our new land.......we will live free like the kings........and tomorrow we will get gold and diamonds out from the holy land". He heard one of them says "when will launch the rocket, Adam?," Adam said "tomorrow, but we should read the instruction book <u>How to launch a rocket, first</u>"

One of them said "let us read the instructions and sent it now, why should we wait till tomorrow?"Adam said "no, let us celebrate tonight we have enough time"

Adam is their leader and leadership is given to the oldest one, the best in working and he is responsible for anything happens in the ship, they were loved and respected him because he is a wise leader.

King Victor got worried and he returned to the army.

Aleksandaro said "it is serious, if our plan does not succeed, tomorrow, they will launch the rocket.".

The king talking to the army "we should wait till the sunrise, when they open the gates, we will begin to kill them, do not have mercy on anyone, kill them all. they are getting ready, the sun was about to rise, king Victor haven't slept because he was so worried, He ordered them to attack from behind the doors in order not to be seen, one group attack who are outside and another group attack who are inside.

The King convene the army and said "it is the first time for me to lead a war since I came to power and I do not want to lose it. these people came from their land because they finished and destroyed their land's treasures by pollution, greediness and wars, He continued, And they are coming to do the same here, do not allow them to steal our land, it is ours, we will defend it and we will get rid of them , like we did to who came before them "get ready, take your positions, " I do not want to hear any voice till I order you to attack"

They took their positions and they got ready, the sun appeared while they were waiting and suddenly the door is opened and some people went out.

Aleksandaro said "shall we attack now, father? "king Victor said "No I want them all to get outside, there might be someone inside, that he might get armed, He continue talking to the army "kill men before women, I want to see all men dead outside"

They waited till people got outside the ship and the king shouted "attack"

They ran quickly like lightning and the king was in the forefront army.

The coming occupiers were astonished, they did not expect anyone to be living on this planet, most of them were flabbergasted, and the army killed men, then women and children. Adam hurried to the ship and closed the door. king Victor took out the gun and shot him from behind the door, Adam was injured in his chest, there were three persons inside the ship, Aya, David and their mother, Goweil, their mother was checking the water for David before taking a shower and then she went to comb Aya's hair. Aya was seventeen years old, David was fourteen and Goweil was fifty seven, while their father had died six years before their arrival, he was fifty eight years old then. They heard the shot's sound .Goweil said "what is this sound?"She went to the door and her daughter Aya found Adam lying on the ground, dying

Goweil said to Adam "what happened?" Adam said "it seems that they are the land owners, they are armed, they killed all who were outside Adam continued "take this key, it is the key of weapons safe downstairs go and launch the satellite rocket and...." then Adam died. Adam wanted to tell her to send a message to the earth to tell

them that there are people living there but he died. Goweil said
"what to do? And how to launch the satellite rocket how.. How?"

Suddenly Victor's army began to hit the door with catapults blow
after blow. Aya cried, her mother hugged her. Goweil did not find
any other choice except defending her children. She went to her son
David, he was wearing his clothes, she pulled him from his hand,
and David said "what is going on?".his mother hugged him and said
"some people have attacked us and killed all who were outside and
they now want to break the door to enter and kill us" David cried,
they went to the bottom of the ship, they found a big safe, she opened
it with the key, she found five machine guns, a pistol and many shots
.she took the pistol, put the ammunition and she took some shots. She
was searching for a safe place to hide her children. She did not find
anywhere except a hole of ventilation. She hugged them, they were
crying, she said "Hash do not cry, I will be back but don't make any
sound. She opened the ventilation pipe from the upstairs then put
Aya and David. And told them "don't speak don't make any voice".

Goweil went upstairs, she heard the door breaking while they were
hitting with catapults and she was at the passage. They broke the
door, the army entered with King Victor. exchange of fire began,
they were all killed one after another, King victor shot her and she
also shot him but in his shoulder and she ran away to the room and
closed it to fill the pistol but they broke the door.

The king killed her with the pistol and Goweil died.

The king fell on the ground injured and Aleksandaro was crying for
his father, King Victor said while he was happy" we won, my son.
Take her weapon and mine and inspect the ship, then bring it to the
empire. Aleksandaro said "Father, let us burn it". The king said" no,
not now but later because there are many things that we want inside,
we need everything..Weapons, books, medicines and iron .we should

get them then we will burn it. other people may come and we should benefit from what's inside it then he said "if I died, Take care of your people guard them with your life and do not forget your sister, make her the king's vice and tell her that I love her "Prince Aleksandaro cried and said "with due obedience, father". Aleksandaro said to the guards "come on, take my father to the empire quickly and call a doctor for him "he ordered some guards and said "inspect the ship well and search for people and do not tamper it and do not touch things" 10 guards entered, inspecting it , king Victor on the way to the empire and Aleksandaro was saying good bye to his father, he was sad about his father, and the soldiers who died.

Aya and David heard someone saying "there is another way to the bottom" 5 people went down stairs, they were running towards the room and they entered the room and searched it. One of the guards saw the safe opened, he opened it and said "what is this? He took a machine gun and he asked one of the guards "what is this?" one of the guards said "Prince Aleksandaro said "do not touch anything but search for people I think it is clear, come on put down the gun or I will tell the king and let us go upstairs, there is nobody here "he put the machine gun in the safe and they went back upstairs then out of the ship to the prince Aleksandaro and said "we did not find anyone inside" Aleksandaro said to some guards" go and bring all slaves and servants to pull it" prince Aleksandaro put guards at the gate entrance of the ship in order not to be stolen. He put 10 guards in shifts for guarding the ship and told them "do not let anyone in, there are spoil inside"

Inside, there were Aya and her brother, they were afraid, crying they do not know that their mother has died , David was saying to his sister "I am afraid, I want my mother"

After a day and a half, they felt thirsty and hungry, Aya said I will bring some food pills and water and search for my mother, wait for me here and never get out. She opened the ventilation hole and said to her brother "close it "she saw the opened safe and the key was on it . She closed the safe and took the key and she went crawling to the room that contains water and food pills. She heard the guards outside, singing and celebrating victory and she went towards the feeding pills and water store, she was near to the ship's door. she was afraid, she opened the safe and there were feeding pills inside, she took the pills and a plastic jar of water, she filled it, she was very confused and frightened she heard their voices close to her while she was getting out, the water jar fell .one of the guards heard the sound and he entered the room, he did not find anyone, he found the water spilled on the ground and he found a jar of plastic on the ground. Aya was hiding in a small drawer, he kept searching the room and the drawers and then when he reached the drawer that Aya is inside, another guard entered, he said "what are you doing here? Prince Aleksandaro ordered not to touch it". The guard said "I have heard a sound in the room ". The other guard said "do not worry ,there is no one here, we have searched everywhere even the cupboards. Come on, get out" he said "look at the spilled water on the ground ". The other guard said "May be it was here before". Aya was afraid, she put her hand on her mouth, her heart was shivering strongly. She waited till their voice disappeared and they began to sleep. she opened the cupboard and crawled she heard the voice of 3 people talking with each other at the ship's entrance, she took the jar of water and filled it and left the room , she was shivering till she reached the room where her brother was hiding, she called her brother with a faint voice but he did not reply, she was afraid that he may be died, she pulled a chair that was at the room and climbed it

Then climbed at the hole, her brother was sleeping, she woke him, and when he saw her, he cried and hugged her, and said "where were you? I was worried about you, did you see my mother?". She said "no" and she did not know that her mother died in one of the rooms, she gave him water and some pills and he hugged her and slept.

While king Victor was on his way to the empire, he was bleeding, he cried and looked at the sky and said "I did it for you, my beloved wife, now come and take me to live with you in the sky and he was watching a light coming from the sky and the last thing he watched was that Sofia descending from the sky and opening her arms to him then, he fainted, he was bleeding a lot . he reached the empire fainted, guards hurried up and put him in bed, Emilia was crying, the doctor arrived and examined him and said to Emilia "he is bleeding a lot, he Stitched the wound and put some herbs on it, and said to Emilia" let him drink milk

after few days, workers started to move the ship , Aya said" to her brother "it is moving, they are taking it," they felt its movement and the voices of the workers, while they were pulling it and after months, the ship reached the empire gate with great celebration, a lot of people gathered to see the victory and they were shouting "long live the king, long live the king, then Aleksandaro hurried to see his father, he had a coma, He is not up yet.

 After some weeks, Aleksandaro went inside in the ship with some guards . They went to the bottom and entered the room, the prince Aleksandaro saw the safe, he said "bring all the blacksmiths tomorrow and break the iron door, it seemed that it is a safe for weapons or precious things" then they left.

Aya heard Aleksandaro's words, she get out of the ventilation hole and opened the safe quickly and started to give her brother the weapons to put them in the hole and after that the ammunition and then closed the safe.

Aya knows that if she did not escape today, she would stay for
months, squeezed inside and that they should escape now whether it
is daylight or night, she gave her little brother food pills, she put
them in his pocket and saw from the window that it was night, she
saw the palace and some soldiers spreading everywhere, they went
out from the ship gate, they were crawling, Aya said to her brother
"we will walk by the wall till we find the gate and get out, they were
sneaking by the wall till they watched the gate, there were 4 guards
and beside the gate she saw a barn where there are many horses.
Aya said to her brother David "follow me to the barn", they entered
the barn, it was big and there was a room full of straw from horses
feeding, where they slept there their first night outside the ship and
in the early morning while they were sleeping, Aya woken up by the
sound of the horses standing in front of the palace and the guard
was saying "come on, bring the water seller has brought water to the
palace, she stood hurrying and watched from a hole between wood
in the barn and the water seller was descending water and
transferring it to the palace. Aya woke her brother and she said to
him "there is a water cart , we should escape in it before anyone find
us. She waited till he descended the last barrel of water and they
went out sneaking and got into the water cart. She heard the water
seller saying "I have descended all barrels of water and I want my
salary" the guard said "well, I will tell prince Aleksandaro and he
will give you your salary next time "

he rode his horse and went out of the palace, Aya and her brother
David were in the cart and after sometime the cart stopped and she
and her brother get off it quickly but the feeding pills that were in
her brother's pocket dropped on the ground and they escaped.

At their first day in the empire, David entered his hand in his pocket
and said to Aya "the feeding pills are not with me "she said "do you
remember the last time they were with you" he said "no, last thing I
remember is that when you put them in my pocket, perhaps it

171

dropped while I was sleeping or in the water seller's cart. A day passed, Aya and her brother no longer have any food or money. They slept their first night at the street. People were giving them little food and at the second day, they were at the market without food, they were searching for food, her brother became pale and he could not walk.

Aya said "do not be afraid, my brother..I will bring you some food she left him on the ground in front of a pottery shop and went.

She was searching for a person to give her food or money and she saw a baker putting bread on the table, it was fresh and hot, she said "please I want some bread "

He said "pay five silver coins".

She said "I do not have money, I beg you, I have a brother, and he will die if I didn't feed him".

He said "I have a whole family if I did not feed them, they will die, go away".

She stood at the baker's door and cried, the baker was busy with a customer, she entered her hand and stole some bread and then she ran away, the baker saw her.

He ran after her and shouted "stop the thief" he caught her from her hair while he was shouting "thief ...thief".

She was crying "please, please, sir my brother is dying of hunger please".

The guard said "what is going on? "

The baker said "she has stolen a piece of bread and ran away but I caught her".

The guards took her and she was saying "please my brother will die".

The guards said "you will say this to the king" the guards entered and Aya with them.

Prince Aleksandaro said "who is this girl and what is her story?"

The guard said "she has stolen bread from the baker and ran away".

King Aleksandaro said "come, little girl" and she was crying" why do you steal and you know that the punishment of stealing is prison".

She said "sir, we did not eat for two days and my brother fainted because of hunger and I asked for people's help but no one wanted to help me. I do not want food I only want my brother to eat and live he is young".

Prince Aleksandaro felt sorry about her, he said "where is your parents?"

She said "they died and I am an orphan, all that I have is my brother, please sir if I am late, my brother may die of hunger please let me give him bread and then you can send me to the prison "she was crying.

The King gave her money and said "I will forgive you this time only because you are little, , go and I do not want to see you here again"

she said "thank you, your majesty "she got out and went hurrying to bring some food to her brother, she bought bread for her and him and she went to her brother's place, but she did not find him. "Where is my brother" the owner of the pottery shop said "I think he died, someone saw him lying on the ground and he carried him".

She cried and said "where did he go with him? And do you know him ?"he said "no, but perhaps he took him to the doctor" she started to ask everyone and she did not find him, she spent a whole week searching for her brother but in vain, the bread and money that she has had finished.

One day she was standing in front of a tavern, the innkeeper saw her and got near her and offered her food and she started to eat quickly because of hunger.

The innkeeper said "do you want more food?"

She said "yes"

He said "do you want to work with me?"

Aya said " what is the type work?

He said "it is easy and simple also you will get money as well as daily food "

She said "I want to see what is my work?"

she entered the tavern and he pointed by his hands and said "to stand in the middle and you dance a little and this is the work and do not be afraid, no one dares to touch you "she was frightened and he continued "come on try it and dance if you do not like it, you can go "he held her hand and went to the dance place and she started to dance, she was afraid and confused, people were clapping, only five people were there. She did not like the work .she stopped dancing and then went out.

The innkeeper caught her. He said "what is wrong? Do not be afraid, take this your money for today's work. She said "but I haven't danced a lot".

He said "no, you danced and we enjoyed, they liked you and your dance a lot. Come back here whenever you need money"

She went away and after two days, the money ran out, she heard the announcement of King Victor's death. king Victor was buried and Aleksandaro and Emilia were sad on parting their father and after the third day, it was the of coronation of the king Aleksandro, king of the great empire and celebration was at the palace, Aya saw people walking towards the palace and was asking them "what is going on?"

they said "today is the coronation of the new king and there will be food and drink for free "she went with them and she entered the palace and she was searching among people perhaps, she could find her brother, king Aleksandaro went out and people were clapping and greeting their new king, he was sad for the death of his father. he said "my king and your king had died, he died defending this empire, he told me while he was smiling "get victory for us, my son, take care of your people, defend them by your life and I am here to fulfill his will, by protecting you and fighting for you.(people are clapping and saying long live the king, the protector of the empire. King Aleksandaro shed tears and said "thank you all you may continue the celebration"

The army headed, waving flags and after that with heads on piles. Aya saw her mother and all who were in the ship with her, she went out from the palace crying she said "I will not forget your revenge, they have betrayed you and I will betray them as they did but I have to find my brother first, she searched for him everywhere, in every house, she asks about her brother but to no avail, till she despaired.

After days, she felt hungry and she no longer has money, she returned to the tavern and told the innkeeper "I want to work"

The innkeeper said "with a condition is to complete dancing till midnight".

she agreed and at her first day, she began dancing, people started to annoy her and catch her hands and legs and hug her and she stopped dancing a little, she was looking at the innkeeper...... he got closer to her and said "you will be used to see this but do not worry, no, one will hurt you and this is a promise ..come on, continue, she continued till midnight, he gave her money and food, she was going to sleep outside", he said "wait, it is very cold outside and you may become sick, come with me, he opened the door of one of the rooms, and said "this is your room, if you like it you will pay a simple wage and if you are afraid here, there is a latch to close the door and no one will disturb you. What do you think?"

Aya agreed ,she does not have any other choice. He took a little money from her. She was thinking about her brother and cries "where are you, my brother. Are you alive or dead?"

Months passed. Aya became a famous dancer and the tavern got crowded every night, it made a lot of money to the innkeeper, some taverns were closed because many people stopped going except to this tavern, , this tavern became number one in the empire

Two years later, Aya have a lot of money that is enough to live the rest of her life without dancing and stay away from the drunk people

One day, she told the innkeeper "I will stop dancing" the innkeeper got angry and said "what do you say, are you mad ? Why?"

She said "I have earned a lot of money that is enough for me and you told me that whenever I liked to stop dancing, you will agree"

He said "this was before, but now you do not need money but I still need money, you are the source of my money to me and to this tavern.

She said "I am sorry, I am going now"

He said "O guards of the tavern, do not let her go out and stand in front of the door"

She looked at him and said "this was not as we agreed before"

He said "I had broke this agreement, you will not go, you will live here till I allow you to go, after I earn a lot of money and become wealthy"

she said "I will shout and gather the empire's guards, he told the tavern guards to take her inside a room and they tied her with a piece of cloth and he whipped her till she fainted, Aya woke from the coma and her body was blue and she was full of pain she couldn't move

He entered and said" this time, I had punished you ,but next time I will use a knife to cut your head but before that I will .... and he touched her body "you know what I can do, but I have mercy on you and I do not want to hurt you "the innkeeper closed the tavern for three days until she recovered, then he opened the tavern and people were waiting outside at night, work began, he entered, found her wearing make-up and got closer and said "as we agreed if you want to live, stay here till I have a lot of money and then go to hell", he went out and said "let's welcome the dancer, Aya and the audience shouting" Aya Aya Aya ".

Aya entered and drums began to play and she began dancing, it lasted for three years and she kept asking him "did you have enough money"

He said "I am about to collect a wealth, will become wealthy and everyday she asks the same question,

One day he said "this is the last week for you and then you will stop dancing and become free "she was happy and after a week he said "no, it is the next week and he stayed swearing it is the last week.

One day, two persons passed by the tavern. One of them wondered about the tavern and what was happening inside it: "Why are people crowded here?" His friend answered: "It's the most famous tavern all over the Empire, the most beautiful dancer works in it. Let's have a look". But the first man did not agree to enter the tavern calling it as a shithouse. However, the man who suggested entering the tavern tried to convince his friend that they would not stay a long time and that they would only watch the dancer then leave immediately: "We will just see how the dancer is. People say that she is charming"

They entered the tavern where there was a beautiful dancing girl surrounded by drunk dancing men who were throwing money to her. The two friends came nearer to the dancer who stopped as soon as she saw them, she cried: "David! Brother!" David did not believe that his sister became a dancer. His friend asked about if David knew her. Aya hugged David while the drunk men were holding her clothes shouting for her to continue dancing, she kicked one of them and went to her room with her brother and locked the door leaving the drunk man falling to the ground.

Aya hugged her brother and started crying saying: "My dear brother, I miss you so much. I thought you were dead. You became very old". David said: "I cannot believe that my sister became a dancer and has a room in the tavern". She said: "Brother, I'm just a dancer no more. No one dares to enters my room"

David: "I wish if I saw you in another place; not in this shady tavern dancing"

Aya said: "I didn't found neither place nor work but this; I found no food, no money, and no place to sleep in; I was going to die"

David: "Haven't you found any other job?! You would have been better to work as a servant, or even die of coldness, and ..."

Then he stopped talking

Aya said: "I needed money"

David: "Money...Fuck money!"

And he stood up, get out some money of his pocket, and through the money at her

She fell to the ground crying: "Please, my brother, don't be harsh on me. I cannot believe that you are alive; I thought you were dead"

David: "Yes, I'm now dead"

He opened the door at which there was a drunk man knocking saying: "Come on, baby. Let's have fun". The dancer's brother pushed him inside the room saying: "I paid for you"

She rose, pushed the drunk man away and ran to her brother saying: "Please, brother, come back, don't leave me"

David: "Don't say 'brother'" then he went out angrily with his friend who asked: "Who was that girl? I heard her calling you 'brother'" but David said: "I'll tell you later"

Aya ran after her brother however the bodyguards of the tavern caught her; she was hitting them saying: "leave me; stay away from me; I want to go with my brother", she was shouting: "brother, brother"

David looked behind and found the guards were beating his sister while she was shouting: "brother, brother" and then they compel her to enter into the tavern.

His friend asked him about the girl: "She was saying 'brother', is she really your sister?!"

David: "No, she is not my sister, we grew up together and she was like my sister" he continued: "Please, don't ask me about her anymore and don't tell anyone about her, especially my parents"

He went to his house then he entered his room and cried blaming himself for being cruel to his sister; Aya. He could not sleep all the night remembering the bodyguards of the tavern beating her while she was shouting 'brother, brother' and crying for being miserable.

The owner of the tavern entered Aya's room and asked her about what had happened; he was not in the tavern at that time; he asked her: "What happened? Why did you try to escape?"

Aya: "Please, let me go; my brother came and saw me dancing then he left angrily. I tried to catch him but the guards prevented me"

The tavern owner:" Well, I promise you that it is just one week then you can go freely"

Aya knew that he is lying and that he is greedy so he would not let her go at all. She took her money, tied them into a piece of cloth and put the cloth to her neck; it was too heavy; she had a lot of money.

She opened the door of her room and saw the drunk men in the hall while the bodyguards were dinking at the gate; she closed the door again and thought about a plan to escape.

In the bathroom, she found a small and narrow window that she could not go through. She decided to escape through the gate.

Aya came out from the bathroom and went near to the main door, one of the drunk men said: "The pretty Aya came, come to dance for us; it's the beginning of the night"

She said: "Well" and pretended that she would go to the stage and then she ran quickly towards the gate, kicked one of the bodyguards who fell to the ground and came out from the gate. The bodyguards caught her then they beat and pull her while she was shouting asking for help. Two soldiers came wondering: "What is happening there. Leave her now"

Aya crying: "They held and beat me. Arrest them, please"

The tavern owner: "She is a liar, sir. She stole money from the tavern then she escaped"

The soldiers asked: "Is that true, girl"

Aya: "No, it is not true, they are liars "

The tavern owner: "inspect her; she had steal all my money"

The soldiers ordered her to stop in order to be searched and they already found a large bag that has money with her. They asked her: "Is this money for you?"

Aya: "Yes, sir"

The tavern owner: "Is that believable! Does a dancer can gather a huge sum of money like that! Believe me, sir; it's mine"

The soldiers: "If the problem had not been solved here, we would have taken you to the prison in order to be judged by the king"

The tavern owner: "I agree. I have witnesses"

The bodyguards: "We witness that she stole the money and escaped"

One of the soldiers: "If she gives you the money, do you forgive her and let her go?"

The tavern owner: "Yes I do"

The soldier: "What is your opinion, girl? Do you agree to give them the money in order to end the problem or go to the prison and been judged by the king tomorrow?"

She threw the money to them and said: "Here is your fucking money; I don't want to take it"

The tavern owner laughed saying: "I told you 'just for this week', however you did not believe me". Then he looked at the bodyguards: "Come on, guys. Let her go"

Aya sat down on the ground crying. The guards felt that she was oppressed; they wondered why not she agreed to go to the king as she was honest.

Aya: "I didn't see my brother many years ago, and tonight, my brother came to the tavern and he became angry when he knew that I am a dancer and then he left; I want to search for him before he goes away. Besides, I was afraid of being jailed and then I could not meet my brother forever"

William; one of the soldiers, asked her: "Do you have a house?"

Aya: "No"

William: "It's too cold here; you would die if you didn't find a warm place for sleep. What about coming with me to my house where I live with my mother; you can stay with us till you find your brother"

Aya: "You are very generous"

William said to his fellow: "I will show her my house and come back immediately"

They went to William's house where William's mother was sleeping, he called his mother and when she wake up, he told her that he found a homeless girl and that he offered her to stay in their house because it was too cold.

William's mother welcomed Aya and showed her the room where she would have stayed saying: "This is your room. Just call for me if you need anything. The bathroom is in front of the room. Good night"

Aya could not sleep; she was very depressed; she was thinking about the tavern owner and her brother who gave up her.

David could not sleep also; he rose up and put on his clothes, his mother asked: "David, where will you go? It's too late."

David: "I feel annoyed, I'll come back soon"

His mother: "Don't be late, son. Take care"

David: "Ok"

David went to the tavern looking for Aya. When he asked the tavern owner about her he replied:

"We just kicked her out"

David: "Where did she go?"

The tavern owner: "I don't know. Search for her around the streets"

He went out of the tavern searching for her in vain till morning. He returned back to his house sad and he felt remorse for giving up his only sister.

Aya helped William's mother in house working and searched for her brother in her spare time. Months later, William's mother became ill and Aya cared for her so William was grateful to Aya. One day, William was sitting at his mother's bed when she suggested that

William marries Aya: "William, my son, why don't you marry Aya; she is a kind girl and she always helps me; marry her if you love me"

William: "Mom, I love you and through all my life I haven't disobeyed you; but ..." (He stopped talking for a while)

His mother: "She is a good girl;. Please, my son, I am afraid of dying before I did not have attended your wedding party"

William kissed his mother's head saying: "As you like, Mom"

His mother: "Then, call for her, I want to talk to her"

William calling for Aya: "Aya, come here, please, my Mom wants to talk to you"

William's mother: "Sit down"

Aya sat down besides the mother who said: "My son wants to marry you; what is your opinion?"

Aya to William: "I want to talk to you separately, please"

William went out of the room with Aya who said: "You know that I am dancer"

William: "you were dancer; you left the tavern and began a new life quitting the past"

Aya crying: "I wish if my brother knows that. When he saw me, he did not help me to start a new life; instead, he left me alone"

William's mother was very happy, she said: "God bless your marriage"

They had a simple wedding party, and in the wedding night; William found Aya virgin. He was very happy and he asked her: "How could you still virgin all these years?!"

184

Aya: "Every night, I prayed to God so as to save me of being rapped as they tried to rap me many times, however, I believed that God would protect and save me. I always knew that God knows that I was compelled to work as a dancer and that I needed money"

William kissed her head and hugged her

Months later, the city bells rang, people gathered, and it was announced that king Alekhandro had a baby and a great ceremony would be held in the palace square the next day and food and drink would be presented for free. William asked Aya to go with him to the ceremony but Aya refused to leave his mother alone. William asked his mother to go with them to the ceremony as food and drink are presented for free; she agreed to go.

At the palace square, there was a great crowd of people attending the party of honoring Alekhandro; Victor and Sophia's son. Trumpets knocked declaring that the king would overlook from the balcony.

Once the king overlooked the balcony, all people clapped and shouted: "Long Live Alekhandro, Long live Alekhandro" while he was waving his hand greeting them. Then, he waved for them to stop and started talking:

"I named my baby after my father Victor who sacrificed a lot to save you from the occupiers who wanted to steal your land, riches and gold, however, Victor, my father, has defeated them and we will send their corpses to their leaders using the spaceships by which they come here"

All people clapped shouting: "Long live the King, Long live the King"

He continued: "I became the King of the Empire and my sister, Emilia, became a viceroy according to our father's will"

185

All people: "Long live the King, Long live Emilia; long live the King, Long live Emilia"

Alekhandro put the crown to Emilia's head while William and his mother were clapping of joy, however Aya was crying; she remembered her mother and friends who were on the spaceship. William asked her: "Why don't you clap? Why are you crying?"

Aya: "I just remembered my brother. I wish he was here"

The King: "Now, Emilia, will speak"

Emilia: "Thank you. My brother said what I was going to say about my dear father whose sacrifice will not be forgotten. I wish I were fighting with our army, however, my father refused to leave the Empire without a ruler. May God bless and protect us"

Emilia continued: "There is happy news for you. I will establish the first school to learn reading and writing; whoever wants to work as a teacher should study the books then he will work in the school and we will pay for him"

Some people said laughing: "What should we do with learning; will it feed us?"

Aya stopped crying and decided that she would revenge; she thought that she would look for her brother as he is the only one who was able to help her. They returned back to their house. After that she went out searching for him.

One day, William gave Aya some money saying: "I am going to work, buy bread for us"

She went to the market and while she was wandering in it, she met David's friend who was with him in the tavern; she caught him to ask about her brother;

186

David's friend: "Who are you?"

Aya: "Please, where is my brother, David?"

David's friend: "I remembered you. You are the dancer"

Aya: "Yes, It's me. Please tell me where he is"

David's friend: "I cannot; he may get angry with me"

Aya: "Please, it's an urgent matter"

David's friend: "I am sorry, I cannot. If he wanted to see you again, he would have returned to the tavern to look for you"

Aya: "Please, tell him that I look for him and that I live in that house"

David's friend: "Ok. I will do"

He left here; however, she decided to watch him till she knew his house in order to return back to him so as to convince him to tell her brother about her place. After he finished shopping, he went to his house and she walked behind him till he entered the house then she returned back to her house.

One week later, she went to his house to ask him if her brother knew that she was looking for him. She knocked the door and when he saw her, he asked: "Why are you here?"

Aya: "I want to know my brother's reply"

David's friend: "He don't want to see you anymore"

Aya: "Well, please, tell him to forgive me. Tell him also that I've got married and that I love him so much"

David's friend: "Well, I'll do, go then"

After he closed the door, she heard someone saying: "I'll leave now"

David's friend: "No, don't go out now"

The person inside: "I have an important work, I should leave now"

He opened the door and found his sister at the door;

Aya: "Brother!"

David hugged her strongly and said: "Aya, I'm sorry, I was cruel to you. Oh, as if I see our parents"

David's friend: "I'm sorry; I thought you don't want to see her. Excuse me", then he entered his house.

David: "Come with me"

They walked while talking together; Aya said: "I quitted the tavern"

David: "I know; I went there to look for you and they told me that they kicked you out. I spent that night searching for you wandering in the streets and in the morning I returned home"

Aya cried saying: "They stole my money and threw me in the street, and then a gentleman who works as a soldier took me to his house where I lived with him and his mother and after months he married me"

Aya continued: "What about you? Where did you go that day?"

David: "The last thing I remember is when we were walking through markets; I could not see anything; you said you would have gone to bring food for me. After that I found myself in a strange house where strange people live, they cared for me. Now, I work a carpenter with my father and my mother is a very good woman. I did not feel strange. The person you saw with me before is my brother"

Aya: "Did your brother tell you that I was looking for you?"

David: "No, he did not. I was so angry that I told him not to talk to me about you again and that I did not want to see you anymore"

Aya: "I wonder what he thinks of me"

She continued: "Why did not you search for me?"

David: "I swear that I searched for you every day after work. I looked for you in the market and I was waiting for you in the same place where you lost me"

Aya: "have you attended the coronation of the King?"

David: "No, I was ill"

Aya: "I saw the heads of my mother and all the persons who were in the spaceship hanged on poles; the soldiers carried the poles and wandered with them while people were throwing stones and spitting on them"

David was shocked; he said: "It was a good thing that I could not attend the ceremony; if I attended, I may have been jailed or killed. I swear, if I were there I would have killed them all"

Aya: "I want to revenge my mother"

David: "How could we revenge our mother while the soldiers spread all over the Empire, believe me, we would die if we try to enter the spaceship"

Aya: "Are you dodging?"

David: "No, I swear, my heart is burning of anger; I cannot forget that day"

Aya: "I'll think about some plan; the most important thing is that I found you. Do you want to come with me in order to see my husband and his mother and have lunch with us?"

David: "Yes, I love that. I'll tell my mother that I would go with you"

He entered his house then he came out and said: "My mother wants to see you"

She entered the house and greeted his mother who said: "David talked about you a lot; I am pleased to meet you. Thanks to God because you're together again"

Aya: "Thank you"

Aya and Victor went to the house of Aya where Victor saw William and his mother; they were friendly to him. After sometime he left and Aya was very happy and she thanked God a lot for answering her prayers"

One day, Aya was wandering in the street when she heard a crier declaring that Emilia, the viceroy, would open the first school inside the palace and whoever wanted to join it would learn freely. People were laughing at this saying that there is no need to learning.

Aya went to her brother: "Did you hear the news?" she said "They opened a school"

David: "We had studied enough in the spaceship. I memorized all the books"

Aya: "The school is inside the palace. We'll go there pretending that we don't know anything about the books after that we should think about some plan to inter the spaceship in order to take the weapons for revenge"

She continued: "I want to be a princess and I want you to be the King. Do you agree with me?"

They shake their hands agreeing on what she said then she added: "Revenge and governance or death"

Aya said to her husband that she wanted to join the school but he refused to let her saying that his mother is old and ill and she needed Aya all the time. However, Aya said that William's mother could go with her every day for some time then they return back.

William: "Impossible, my mother cannot walk all that distance every day. What is the benefit of joining that school?"

Aya: "Princess Emilia will give rewards for whoever would apply"

William: "How much is the reward? I'll pay it for you provided you stay at home; my mother needs you"

Aya: "I'm sorry, I'll join the school"

William: "Then, go, but don't come here again"

William's mother came out of her room wondering about what is happening, William said: "Ask her"

She asked Aya gently about what had happened and Aya told her. She told Aya not to worry about her and that she could manage her requirements; she also told Aya that she would convince William to agree. However, William told his mother that it was his decision and that he would not back off.

Aya: "I'm sorry. I'll go tomorrow"

William: "Then, you should take your luggage with you and don't return back to here again"

In the morning, Aya went to her brother and told him what happened, David was angry, he told her that his father did not agree at first, but, he told David that it is his decision and that he is a man who knows what is good for him.

Aya and David went to revenge. There were about 10 persons including Aya and David. Princess Emilia was the teacher; she explained what science is and that it is the basis of life, she showed that there is a difference between educated and non-educated people. Emilia said also that she would explain what exists in the books in order to be civilized persons and that she would show them the evil bearer that was a kind of science. She told them that they may make another one after they study the books.

Aya smiled and winkled to David. They went out of the palace and Aya was very happy; she said: "I cannot wait to see the spaceship"

David: "Come with me; you don't have a place to stay; come and share my room"

They entered David's house; he told his family that his sister wanted to live in their house till she find a place to live and that she would sleep in his room and they welcomed her.

Aya and David went every day to the palace; Emilia was astonished how they understand very quickly; she asked: "How can you understand the lessons quickly, I spend two months analyzing and explaining a question"

She admired them more every day; they were discussing about some questions in mathematics, physics, and other books and they convinced her all the time.

One day, Princess Emilia said: "Next week, I'll make a surprise for you; I'll show you the evil bearer, I've asked King Alekhandro for permission"

Aya held her brother's hand; she was very excited

Emilia gave rewards for Aya and David as they were superior learners.

Emilia said: "I'll establish a school and you who will teach people"

At the day which Aya and David waited for so long; Aya and David were about to carry out their plan to kill the King and the Princess and take over the palace to revenge for their mother and all other people who were on the spaceship.

Emilia entered the room and said: "King Alekhandro permitted us to enter the evil bearer just for few minutes in order to show you how science is a very important thing and that the books could help us build another one like that".

In the evil bearer, there was a surprise; there were about 40 soldiers waiting for them. Aya looked to her brother wondering about what they should do?

David: "I don't know. We have to postpone the plan"

Aya: "It's our chance. They won't permit us to enter the spaceship again; haven't you heard what she said? It's our first and last visit, please, think about it"

They entered the spaceship where the commander of the guards welcomed them and explained how they seized the two spaceships; the first was in the reign of Queen Tessa; King Victor's mother, while the second was in the reign of King Victor and his son Alekhandro.

They entered the first spaceship, Princess Emilia explained for them; she said: "watch this one then compare it with the other. Look, how did they developed evil bearer2 to be more advanced than evil bearer1; there are some differences". They entered the control room; Emilia said: "This is a control unit through which a person can control the evil bearer and make it fly. King Alekhandro ordered to burn it and take the iron but I refused, I told him that superior persons like you may make a spaceship like this in order to attack the occupiers; however, it may occur after thousands of years" Emilia continued: "Hey, guard, come here, what is this and who made it?"

The guard: "It's probably that God who created it"

Emilia: "Do you believe that this is human made?"

The guard: "No, I don't believe that"

Emilia: "Well, go back to work" She continued: "have you heard that? He does not believe in science"

Aya: "they know this land by science too?"

Emilia: "That's right. I want you also to see the rocket that helped them to reach to our land. There is one rocket in every evil bearer, because of bad luck, this one had been launched and the rocket launching was a message for them to know that there is a life here on our land. But the other rocket has not been launched yet, there are guards everywhere to prevent its launching. Let's go and watch evil bearer2"

They entered evil bearer2 accompanied with some guards; they were wandering in evil bearer2 while Princess Emilia was explaining how evil bearer2 is more advanced than evil bearer1. Aya whispered to David: "Do you have a plan?" But he answered: "No, do you?", she said: "No, we should think quickly, I am afraid and confused"

They entered the room where Aya and David were living in; Aya could not stop crying. Emilia asked Aya: "What is the matter with you?"

Aya: "Nothing, I'm fine"

Emilia: "We can make am evil bearer like this one if we have science, will and determination. They were like us; however, the journey of a thousand miles begins with a single step"

Emilia continued: "Let's have a tour before we leave"

Aya whispered to her brother: "What should we do? It's our last chance"

David: "Be quite, I cannot think about it"

It was forbidden for them get in the control unit of evil bearer2; they were allowed to watch it from outside only.

They passed by the entrance of downstairs part; Aya asked: "What is there in the downward part?"

Emilia answered: "There is a room that has a big safe"

Aya: "I want to see it before we leave"

A guard: "It's a dark room, Your Majesty; there is no light in it"

Princess Emilia: "We'll just have a look"

They went down as Aya said to her brother: "Come on, brother, please, think about a plan"

They entered the semi-dark room while Emilia was explaining how blacksmiths tried a lot till they could open the safe a month later and that they did not find anything inside it.

Aya whispered to David: "You pretend that you are watching the safe and I will close the door as if I watch it from the behind and after the group go outside the room, use the weapons to kill all of them"

The guard: "Time is out. You should go out of the room now"

David was inside the safe and Aya closed its door as if she watches it closely then the guard ordered her to go out.

David came out of the safe in order to breathe, he was holding two loaded machine guns and he took all the bullets.

On their way out of the spaceship princess Emilia asked Aya: "How much time do you think they took to build evil bearers 1 and 2, and you David, what do you think..."

Emilia noticed that David disappeared, "Where is your brother?"

Aya was confused, she said: "He was here", she shouted for him "David, David, where are you?"

Emilia ordered the guards to look for him and suddenly he appeared from behind of the spaceship saying: "I'm here, my sister"

Emilia: "What are you doing there alone?"

David: "I brought these things"

Emilia screamed saying: "These are weapons; they are Andree's people, kill them"

Aya ran to her brother who threw a machine gun to her then they killed all the guards while Emilia escaped to her brother, Victor. She could not talk of gasping and crying. He brought some water to her, but she said: "Andre's people took over evil bearer2; they had weapons and they killed all guards"

Victor was astonished: "We have killed all of them!", then he ordered to ring the city bells to gather the soldiers so as to lay siege around the evil bearer

Victor shouted: "go out now before I burn the evil bearer"

Aya and David closed the gate pointing the guns from the windows. Aya spoke loudly to the king: "move back you and your soldiers too"

The King: "What do you want?"

Aya: "We want to govern this land"

The king said angrily: "The governor of this land must have been lived in it, if you do not go out now, I will destroy the evil bearer which you are in"

The king held a meeting with army leaders; they planned for attack by destroying it using catapults, however, the spaceship was so strong and fortified that it did not be hurt.

The King shouted: "Attack. Burn it"

The soldiers attacked the spaceship while Aya and David were shooting them through the windows"

A leader of the soldiers told the King that the only way to defeat them is to penetrate the gate, but, Aya and David killed all of the soldiers who tried to come close to the gate.

Emilia: "What about the gun? Try it"

King Alekhandro refused to use it. He has 80 bullets, however he said that they will use those bullets for the coming people; he said to Emilia: "Don't worry, we will kill them"

The second day passed and Aya and David were still inside the spaceship trying to kill whoever came near. Aya remembered the rocket in the ship; she went to the control unit, read the instructions, and turned the power on, then the ceiling has been opened and the rocket has been launched to the sky. Then, the King said to his sister that he knew they will need the bullets.

King Alekhandro became angry. An idea came to his mind; he said: "They will die of smoke".

He ordered the leaders to bring all clothes exist in the market and shape it like balls. After that, about 300 soldiers attacked breaking the windows with spikes then another 300 soldiers follow them throwing the burning clothe balls inside the spaceship while Aya and David was killing soldiers. Aya was suffocating of smoke and fire that she could not see her brother. Aya fell to the ground suffocating and David tried to pull her searching for clear place of smoke and fire but he could not, and finally they died.

Emilia continued teaching till there was a generation of educated people. She did not marry; she was teaching people all the time.

She opened the first school in the Empire and gave monthly rewards for teachers. Emilia said: "Aya and David were so much useful to me; they taught me a lot of things"

Emilia gave books to the people in order to learn and become able to face Andre's people.

Chapter3

Earth

First signals from the second spaceship have reached the earth, scientists were so happy by this success. But they didn't receive any call from the new land; they tried to contact the people in the spaceship but to no avail.

Scientists wanted to know why they hadn't received any call.

One of them said: "maybe the new earth is occupied by other creatures or humans or the telephone failed to work through all this distance".

Another one said: "you know that there were more than one phone on the spaceship, how come they all fail, maybe there is a secret on this land, as we have no sign to know that they are alive"

A third one said: "I have a plan, but it needs financial support from the American government, it is to make a huge spaceship with thirty satellites that will be launched one after another along the journey and the last one will be launched from the new earth".

One of them asked: "why do we need all these satellites?" the other answered: "to connect all signals, so we would know all about the situation."

They all agreed about the plan and the new project of the huge spaceship.

NASA submitted a report about the new, big project, but the Government refused to support their project, because it will be so expensive, and there is no sufficient evidence that there is life on the new planet, besides there are no signals from those who traveled there before. Moreover, there are a lot of poor people all over the world and many countries live in abstention, and they need this money.

Scientists agreed that they will wait until the government accepts to support the project, or wait for another president that would accept to support sending the biggest spaceship which will be three times bigger than the ordinary spaceship.

Also the resumption had been refused; the reply was to make it when financial state get better, also USA must support needy people inside USA and the poor people all over the very poor world.

The world now has no oil stock, it had ran out of gas, diamonds and gold, people had stopped using cars they use bicycles, horses and few of them have cars working by electricity, using planes in traveling had become a dream, the airplane ticket price had become more 1000% times than it was before, as the rest fuel of the USA and some great countries storage became very little and only the Army and presidents who use it urgently. People used horses and motorcycles again. Scientists wished that one day a new president would approve their coming project.

After 8 years, a new person became a president of America, and the situation all over the world got worse, the new president was sure that the American scientists were able to find a solution. The most suitable solution at that time was to turn water into energy. Scientists tried to separate hydrogen from oxygen in water. The American president declared that he is ready to support any project in order to save the world.

Scientists submitted their research to the new president; their research was to travel to another planet. However, the president had many questions about the previous space flights; "were the persons who went to the other planet still alive?" The scientists assured that the two satellites had already sent and went around the earth; however, there were no calls from them. The president agreed after one year of thinking and studying the researches : After one year, the scientists were told that the president has approved their project and that the fund of the project would be 20 billion dollars would be divided into 5 annual payments. and He told the scientists "But it would be your last chance to prove that there is life on the other planet, if you failed, It would be a great loss of money and energy, and I would not let you do it again" he continued: "I'll think about the matter then I'll tell you my decision"

Congress objected to the decision of the president. They did not agree to pay that great sum of money to fund a project whose effectiveness was not proved yet while there were greater projects that need that fund; such as: nuclear power and separating hydrogen from oxygen in water. But to no avail.

Scientists were very happy, they started their great project. The biggest spaceship was built; it had laboratories, a small school, a control room and a training hall.

After 10 years, they finished their project. There was a few months to launch the spaceship. They declared the need of 40 volunteers and 10 fans of travelling by spaceships. There were only 34 volunteers, 4 astronauts and 3 young police commandos to train the new born in spaceship children on fighting and using weapons

. There was an agreement that the unmarried astronaut should choose one of the volunteers to marry in order to have children. Every unmarried young man chose an unmarried young woman for marriage and a wedding party was held for them, after that they will be trained to live in the spaceship.

After 8 months of training, the scientists told the volunteers that they would be trained by the army to be fighters. The volunteers were astonished; they wondered if they would be sent to fight. The scientists told them that there would not be a war; however, they should be ready for any emergency. The scientists told them also that it was the last chance to prove that there was another life on the other planet or they forget the idea forever; they added: "You may face monsters or aliens as we see on T.V., all of the persons went before did not return back. Get ready".

The volunteers were well-trained by the American Commandos for one year, then they became ready for traveling. They delivered wireless communication devices, besides; every person had a bag *that contained a machine gun, bullets, grenades, devices for night vision and knives. Those bags were all put into a closet and there should have been given to them hours before landing.*

After one month, the volunteers were about to leave; they went to say goodbye to their families, then they returned to NASA to get in the hugest spaceship, then the countdown started and the spaceship was launched to the new earth.

After 5 years, the crew was working nicely and orderly. Over the 5 years, they launched 5 satellites and some of them had children and started to teach them fighting by making simulation for gun war by rubber bullets through fights in the training hall.

One day, a weird baby was born; his mind grew but his body did not. He was called Lion. His father, Doveir did not tell his wife that his father was a dwarf too. He was afraid of being blamed by his wife who loved her baby so much as much as her husband loved him. The children in the spaceship laughed at Lion, they called him Lion the dwarf. He got used to the insults as his parents supported and encouraged him all the time.

After 20 years, the children grew up and so did their parents. Some of the parents died and others are still alive.

Landing time became close.

Landing Day

Every person took his bag that contained a machine gun, bullets, night speculum, a wireless connection device, grenades, mines, lambs and all devices that may be needed in the emergency cases.

They connected belts, and then the spaceship started landing gradually. It was very heavy and huge and it was moving strongly. Something wrong happened when the spaceship landed on the new earth, it crashed strongly on the land and as a result it was broken from the back and burnt. However, All passengers had lost consciousness out of the surprising accident, the front part of the spaceship crawled into the middle of a river.

One of the passengers was called Hilton; he awakened finding himself sinking, he untied the belt and get out from the lake; he took a deep breath then he get down into the water to catch a girl in order to pull her out of water, then he returned to pull a child then a man and he did that many times till he pull 9 persons out of the lake. He tried to give them a mouth-to-mouth, however, only 3 persons who were still alive. The 3 persons were: Lion the dwarf (29 years old), Jolly (a beautiful young 27 years old girl) and Harry (a black 19 years old guy), besides; Hilton (a handsome strong 33 years old person; Hilton spent his spare time training on heavy lifting). He hurried to the river to bring water in order to wash their heads.

Hilton told them that he would go to watch the other part of the spaceship. When he saw the burnt part he began to cry then he returned to them crying , Jolly asked him about the other passengers; he told her that they are all dead. All of them began to cry; Jolly then Harry, while Lion sat down in shock; his parents were in the same part with him, he cried and so did Hilton. Jolly hurried to the burnt part, she wanted to jump into the spaceship so as to save her parents. She was crying: "I want my parents, I want my parents". Hilton prevented her from entering the burnt spaceship saying that all of them lost their parents. He took her away from the catastrophic scene and went to gather the bags. There was a problem that the food was burnt and so was the ammunition; they had only a little ammunition. Hilton told them that they would stay some time till the fire is over, in order to pull out the burnt bodies so as to bury them after saying the praying. Jolly's hand was burnt after she touches the hot iron. Hilton bandaged her wound. He dug up a grave and buried the 6 burnt bodies including Lion's parents, they prayed for them then they went to sleep till morning to take some rest before they burry the rest of the bodies.

Jolly could not sleep. She was crying over her parents. After the sunrise, she went to the place of the spaceship to see it. When she came closer to the place, she saw a huge number of soldiers on horses gathering around it. She hurried to Hilton who was a sleep. She awakened him up saying: "Hilton, wake up, there is a huge army with horses around the spaceship"

Hilton was scared he asked her: "Are they aliens?"

Jolly: "No, they are humans just like us"

Hilton awakened and took his bag and awakened Lion and Harry to tell them about the army. He told them to hide until he would have a look.

Hilton went to have a look at the army. He watched them by the speculum and then he hurried to his friends saying: "Let's escape, it's very dangerous, the army is so huge"

They escaped through trees till they reached some place, then they hid in. Hilton told them to stay hidden till he would come back. He went to the place of the spaceship in order to watch the army by the speculum. There are soldiers everywhere searching for something as if they know that there is a missing part. They were tracing the crawling of the other part into the river. One of them swam in the river, and suddenly, he shouted: "I found it, it was sunken". After that some workers went to pull that part out of the river while some other workers were pulling the burnt part. Hilton returned to his friends and told them that the army has taken over the spaceship. Harry was angry, he said that he would go to kill them but Hilton cried to him that they have no ammunition to kill the soldiers with. Hilton added that the army would search for them to kill them.

Jolly said to Hilton: "Do you want them to take over the spaceship?!"

Hilton: "No, we would take it back. After they finish pulling it, we'll trace them and we'll find a way to get it back".

They still two months; every day he watch them pulling the spaceship till they became very far. After 6 months, Hilton told them that they must have been arrived; "Let's go, they must have been arrived now"

They traced the spaceship till they reached to the Empire. They stayed away watching. They saw the guards at the gate inspecting everybody enters. Hilton: "We cannot enter, they inspect whoever enters, and moreover, our suits seem to be strange. We should find some clothes and a carriage in order to enter.

They stayed until they found 5 persons on a carriage. They killed them and took over their clothes and carriage; however, there were no clothes for Lion. Hilton cut a suit and wrapped it around Lion's body, and then he tied it with a rope. Hilton told them that they could not enter the city with the weapons; "Let's wander in the city till we think about a way to get the weapons inside"

They dug a hole and put their bags except Jolly, she refused to enter without weapons; she said: "What if we faced any danger? At least I will take a knife and a speculum"

Hilton: "Well, I'll try to hide them under the saddle of the horse"

He hid the knife and the speculum under the saddle then they walked to the gate, Hilton greeted the guards who started searching in the carriage. One of the guards put his hand on the saddle then he touched a piece of iron. He caught it wondering about it; "what is this?" The guard called the other guards to see the iron thing, and then he ordered Hilton and his friends to get down from the carriage. The four friends were jailed in order to be presented to the king.

By the road, Lion said to Jolly: "we'll be executed due to your plan, Jolly"

Hilton: "It's not the suitable time for struggling; we should find a way to save our lives". He continued: "We'll say that we found it at the river when we were fishing"

They were jailed till the king decides to judge them. They stayed one day in the prison then the door of the prison was opened, the guards came and took them to the king.

The king was Jiff, the son of the 2nd. Alekhandro. After Alekhandro has died, his elder brother, Victor became the king till he died of fever. King Jiff is 17 years old and his sister Princess Kathy is 16 years old. Their mother died of sorrow because of her husband's death. After Aleksandro's death, the Empire was sunken in injustice. King Jiff was unserious and unjust; many people described him as a mad man. He was the youngest king of the Empire.

The four prisoners were taken to be presented to the king. When they entered, they were surprised by the king of being the very young. King Jiff was examining the knife and the speculum; he was looking at them through the speculum.

King Jiff asked: " who's these things belong to?"

Hilton: "It's mine, Your Majesty, I found it when I was fishing; we came here in order to give it to you as a present, however, the guards arrested us"

Lion: "Yes, sir, that's right"

The king was astonished; he thought Lion is a child. He came closer to Lion and asked him about his name: "What's your name?"

Lion: "My name is Lion; they call me Lion the dwarf because I'm short"

King Jiff to Hilton: "Is he your son?"

Hilton: "Yes, your Majesty, she is my wife and this is my son too"

King Jiff looked at Harry with amazement; then he looked at them one after another!!! After a period of silence he said: "What a strange family! A beautiful blonde mother, a handsome burly father, a black son and another short one. How come? How could I believe that?"

Hilton: "Could I tell you a secret?"

King Jiff came closer to Hilton who said: "I think my wife is cheating on me with many guys"

King Jiff laughed saying: "Does she cheat on you? Why don't you kill her and kill the short and black boys, too?"

Hilton: "Majesty, if I killed them, I would not find another beautiful wife and I would not find children who can help me; I'm a poor man"

King Jiff: "Do you want me cut her head for you and give you money to marry another woman?"

Hilton: "Your Majesty, I will kill her myself; I want to catch her with her stud as I want to kill him, too"

King Jiff ordered the guards to take them to the prison: "Take them to the prison till I think about a punishment for them"

King Jiff laughed saying: "I've never heard about a strange family like this, even in tales"

King Jiff ordered the guards to leave Lion then he took him to his room and ordered him to take off his clothes. Lion was astonished of that order; however, he did what the king asked. King Jiff laughed saying: "you're a devil. It is bigger than you"

King Jiff brought women for Lion and sat down watching him doing funny movements that made King Jiff laugh in a hysterical way. King Jiff was playing to Lion every day; they became friends and they slept at the same room. After months, King Jiff said to Lion: "You're my friend and I will make you a consultant"

Lion: "It's my honor, your Majesty"

Every week there was one day King Jiff was judging in cases between disputants. One day, a wife came to King Jiff to complain about her husband who did not give her money, and go every night to bars, spent his time with prostitutes, and did not sleep at home most of the time. King Jiff asked her about her husband, and when he came, the King asked him about what his wife said.

208

The man: "No, Your Majesty, she is a liar; I give her enough money for her and our children. This woman is snippy; I swear that I leave the house escaping from her bad behavior. She always blames and insults me in front of presence of our children"

The woman: "What about our money that is being spent on the prostitutes, besides, you don't sleep at home with us"

The man: "Yes, Your Majesty, I do that, however, she who pushes me to sleep away from her to escape from her loudmouth"

King Jiff looked at his consultant Lion asking him about his opinion. It was the first time the King ask him about a consultation.

Lion said: "I feel that the woman is the right one ; you should order him to give her a monthly wage for her and the children"

King Jiff: "Cut his penis and give it to his wife; that's the punishment of cheating on his wife"

The woman cried: "What can I do by his penis; I'm here to ask for his money not for his penis"

King Jiff ordered to Cut her tongue, too, and give it to her husband in order to sleep quietly"

Lion was astonished with that cruel judgment; he stopped talking.

Another person came to complain a third one accusing him of stealing his donkey. King Jiff asked about the accused person who admitted that he already has taken the donkey: "I took the donkey, however, I didn't steal it; I just took what is mine"

King Jiff: "Why did you take the donkey?"

The accused: "The man borrowed a sum of money from me 3 years ago, and whenever I ask him about my money, he says that he doesn't have, and that I should be patient; when I ran out of patience, I took the donkey which I found at his house"

The donkey owner: "I swear, if I had money, I would have given him his money; I bought that donkey in order to use it in transportation so as to give him his money back"

King Jiff looked at Lion asking about his opinion. Lion said: "The accused should give the donkey to its owner provided that he would take it again if he didn't get his money within one year"

King Jiff: "A wise judgment. Cut the thief's hand in order not to take things that don't belong to him, and kill the donkey so that the donkey owner stops borrowing money anymore"

King Jiff looked to Lion and said: "The case is being solved. If we didn't judge that way, they would do that again and come to me here another time. That's the best judgment"

Lion kept quiet and knew that there is no way for his friends to survive.

One day, he was doing funny dances for the king, he was tumbling and dancing naked and jumping above the naked girls. After King Jiff laughed a lot, he said to Lion: "I like you so much, Lion; you pleased me a lot"

Lion: "That pleases me, Your Majesty" and added: "Do you have any friends besides me?"

King Jiff: "I tried, but I didn't find a friend like you. You make me laugh and you accept my humor"

Lion said: If you please your Majesty, I want to see my family.

King Jiff said: "I want to tell you a secret"

Lion: "What is it, Your Majesty?"

King Jiff said: "you should forget about your family. That big man is not your real father, and that black guy is not your brother; your mother is unfaithful; she cheats on your father with other men"

Lion: "Really, I don't believe that. Who told you that?"

King Jiff: "Your father did"

Lion: "Oh my God! I cannot believe that. Please, Your Majesty, let me see them in the prison. I want to be sure about that. It is a serious matter"

King Jiff laughed saying: "Well, Guards, take Lion to see his mother; the bitch"

As soon as July saw Lion, she rushed to him saying: "I swear if you don't find a way for us to get out of here, I'll tell the truth and you'll be thrown into prison with us" she was very angry: "How come you are having fun out of the prison while we are here in"

Lion: "Be quiet, I swear, I did not forget you, however, that king is mad; you don't know how he judges people" then he left.

King Jiff asked him: "did you talk with them about the issue?"

Lion: "Yes, my mother denied all of what was said, and there was a struggle between my mother and father, besides my brother cried when he knew the truth"

After that Lion kneeled before king Jiff saying: "Your Majesty, please, release them"

King Jiff: "Why do you care about them after all this, you became my consultant and I gave you money, women and all what you want"

Lion said: "I don't want them after I knew the truth, however, they would blame me for not helping them as we were one family, please, Your Majesty"

King Jiff: "Well, tomorrow, they will be judged"

The next day, they came to the king who asked his consultant: "What do you think about an unfaithful wife, a fake brother, and a softy father who don't know the truth about his children. Can we judge them?"

Lion think a little then he said: "Kill them all, Your Majesty, I wish if my father kill that bitch and that brother would urinate upon them"

King Jiff laughed hysterically till he has fallen down of his chair.

Hilton, July, and Harry were shocked; they asked Lion about what he said: "Are you crazy?"

King Jiff: "It's a great judgment; I've never heard one like it before"

Then King Jiff said: "Be quiet, be quiet. Lion, I would give your father the chance to know the truth of your unfaithful mother, and the chance is for that black boy to know his real father"

King Jiff continued: "For you, Lion, we will be your family"

King Jiff looked at Hilton, July, and Harry then said: "Go, I forgive you, provided that you are forbidden to go out of the city; also a guard would accompany you all the time, and if you went out of the city, I would judge you like what my consultant said. Go"

When they went out, King Jiff hugged Lion saying: "Well, I want you strong, don't have mercy on anyone"

After a period of time, Lion asked to see his family as he did not see them since they were released. King Jiff permitted him to see them once every month, "Well, you can see them one time every month, but you should go with guards as you are my consultant now"

Lion: "Thank you, Your Majesty"

When Lion met them, July was very angry, she wanted to hit him but the guards prevented her, while Hilton said: "Be quiet, July" then he looked at Lion: "What do you want?"

Lion: "I came here in order to see you"

July: "We don't want to see you again ; have you forgotten what you said for judging us?"

Lion: "you don't know what happens", he came closer to them then he said: "That king is mad; every time I say a fair judgment he ordered to do the contrary that is why I told him to kill you in order not to do so. You're free now because me"

July: "We are not free. Look at that guard, he follows us wherever we go"

Hilton: "Please, July, let me talk" then he said to Lion: "Lion, you are close to the king, try to find us a way in order to get out from here"

Lion said angrily: "Am I a king, I'm just a consultant, I don't have any powers in that fucking Empire"

July: "We don't want his help; I will find a way to get out from here"

Lion: "Do you want to be killed; have you forgotten what the king said?"

July: "Did you forget our true mission? You are having fun with that fool king"

Hilton: "That's enough, July"

"Please, Lion, find us a way to get out from here. Ask the king about the spaceship and where did he bury the dead people on it. I'm sure that you will find a way for us"

Lion gave some money to Hilton and said: "I'll see you next month; the king only permitted me to visit you one time every month. Believe me, I'll think about some way to get you out of here"

After that Lion left with the guards to the palace.

July said: "I'll escape"

Hilton caught here saying: "Are you crazy? We may be killed. We should escape together or the king would kill us if you escaped alone. Couldn't you hear Lion when he said he is a mad king?"

July: "Well, I'll give him a chance till the next month; if he did not find a way to get us out of here, I would escape alone"

Lion went to the palace and met King Jiff who asked him: "have you seen your family?"

Lion: "Yes, Your Majesty"

King Jiff: "Is there any news about them?"

Lion: "Nothing new. My mother insists on denying the entire story. She assures that Hilton is our father"

King Jiff: "I wish if your father made me torture her in order to admit everything, however, he insists on knowing the truth by himself"

King Jiff continued: "Come here, my best friend, I miss you, sit down next to me. Do you want to have fun with girls now?"

Lion: "No, Your Majesty, I'm tired. However, I want to talk with you. I heard about the crash of the strange thing which fell from the sky; what did you do with it and what did you do with the dead?"

King Jiff: "You mean the evil-bearer? Before his death, my father told us that they are some people, coming from another planet, wants to come and steal our land"

Lion: "So, what did you do with them?"

King Jiff: "Some of them were burnt, and the others sunk and became food for fish"

Lion: "Where are the burnt bodies?"

King Jiff said laughing: "Do you think I'm a bad king?! I gave them to wolfs, dogs, and eagles to eat their cocked flesh"

Lion went to bed thinking about a way to convince the king that he wants some money in order to buy a house near to the Empire Fences. Then they would dig a tunnel under the wall so as to get out through it. He went to the king and said: "Your Majesty, I want some money"

King Jiff wondered: "I give you enough money every month"

Lion: "I want the money in order to buy a house for my family; I would not live with them, I'll stay in the palace, just I want to reassure that they live in a house for a monthly rent"

King Jiff: "Well, I'll give you the money but it's the last time that you ask anything for your family; just for you" and he gave Lion the money.

After one month Lion went to see his family after he asked for the king's permission. When he entered, July rushed saying: "Did you find a way for us to get out from here?"

Lion: "I think that I should buy a house for you"

July: "I swear, if it wasn't the guard, I would have cut you, fucking dwarf. What would we do by a new house?"

Hilton: "Please, be quiet till he finish talking"

Lion: "I thought about a plan; I would buy a new house that would be near to the empire fences, then we should dig a tunnel to lead us out of the Empire"

July: "Do you think that they would not hear us digging? And what about that fucking guard who does not let us be alone all the time?"

Lion: "I have no plan but this one. I spent one week thinking about it"

Harry: "I agree with you, Lion"

Hilton: "Well, why don't we try, It seems a good idea. What's your opinion, July?"

July: "I have no choice. I'll try to obey the dwarf; just for this time"

They searched for a house that stuck to the fence. All houses owners didn't agree to sell but there was one who agreed to sell his house expensively. They moved to the new house and the guard still accompanying them. He stood at the door in order not to let them separate; they were permitted only to walk together under his guard.

July thought about how to get rid of the guard. Hilton said: "We should persuade the guard that we will do some decorations for our house, and build a new room"

Hilton went out to the guard and said: "Could you help us in making some decorations, and build a new room in our house?"

The guard said: "Am I a worker! Look at me, I'm a guard, Go search for help away from me, I don't work for you"

Hilton said: "Why don't people help each other?" then he entered the house saying: "I persuaded the guard that we do decoration works and that we want to build a room inside the house"

They chose the nearest room to the wall and started digging. Hilton was digging while Harry and July were putting the dust into an old will which was useless. The guard got used to the digging noise as he believed that they were decorating a building a room in their house. Every night, when they stop digging, they close the hole with wood. They were proceeding in digging. However, there was a big problem that there was a huge rock on the way of digging. They spent 3 weeks thinking about how to break this rock in order to widen the hole more than 3 inches.

July: "Why don't we ask for help from Lion the dwarf? We cannot get in this hole because the width is not suitable for us; however, it is suitable for his short body. He can continue digging and go out in order to bring weapons for us"

Hilton: "We have no choice but that"

They tried digging more but to no avail. The rock hindered them from proceeding. Days after that, Lion came to see them and the guards were with him as usual. When he arrived to the house, he ordered the guards to return back to the palace saying: "You can return back to the palace. I'm with my family; there is no danger"

As soon as he entered, July rushed to him saying: "Well, you are having fun with the king, eating and drinking in the palace while we are working here"

Hilton: "Please, be quiet, July. He did not give up on us; he helped us a lot".

Then he said to Lion: "We need your help"

Lion: "I'm ready"

Hilton: "We want you to continue digging. It's just a short distance to the wall"

Lion agreed provided that he return back to the palace early. He started digging and getting out sand till he became very close to the wall. Suddenly, some sand and rocks collapsed while he was inside the hole. Hilton shouted: "Lion, Lion" and tried to dig with his hands in order to catch him. Scarcely, he caught his toes, but he could not pull him. He said: "July, Harry, let's pull him"

July: "Well, I'll bring something to pull him"

Hilton, July and Harry pulled Lion till they get him out of the hole. He was unconscious and all his body was bloody. They put him on the bed, they thought he was dead. July said: "I'll bring a doctor". Suddenly, the door knocked; they were the guards of the king asking for Lion. July said: "I didn't see him. He went to the palace few hours ago"

The guard who watches them said: "No one came out of the house"

The guards pushed her and entered the house searching for Lion who was completely bloody. When the guards saw him on that case, they cried and wielded their swords. They thought that Lion was killed. They arrested the three friends and took them to the prison, and then they took Lion to the palace.

King Jiff cried when he saw Lion completely bloody. He ordered the guards to bring a doctor immediately. After few hours, Lion opened his eyes, while King Jiff was crying saying: "Please, don't leave me, my friend, don't die"

Lion: "Where am I?"

King Jiff: "You're in the palace. What happened?"

Lion: "I don't remember anything"

King Jiff: "I swear to God, I'll punish them. I'll kill them brutally"

Lion: "If you love me, don't hurt them"

King Jiff's sister, Princess Kathy was in love with someone called Ethan. She meets him out of the palace. He is about 17 year's old, same age of King Jiff. She knew him when she was studying in the school of the palace as her father Alekhandro compelled her and her brother on studying. King Jiff and his sister's beloved young man did not like each other, as once King Jiff saw him kissing his sister; King Jiff then became so angry and he took an oath that if he saw Ethan with his sister again, he would kill him and punish his sister. However, Alekhandro solved the problem by expelling him out of the palace school and building another one in the Empire.

One day, King Jiff asked about his sister, the guard said that she went out walking as usual and that the maids accompanied her.

King Jiff: "I'm bored because Lion is ill; I'll go after her so as to walk together, where did she go?"

The guard: "She is in the market"

King Jiff went to the market. He found Princess Kathy talking with Ethan. King Jiff asked them angrily: "What are you doing?"

Princess Kathy: "I met him accidently. He was just greeting me, if you don't believe me, ask the maids"

219

King Jiff asked the maids: "Is that true?"

The maids: "Yes, that's right"

He went angrily to the palace. He called for one of the maids and said: "Tell me the truth or I will kill you"

The maid crying: "Do you ensure me that Princess Kathy would not hurt me"

King Jiff: "Yes, I do. Tell me now"

The maid: "They used to meet each other every week and walk alone; she gave us money in order not to tell you"

King Jiff became very angry; he shouted on the maid: "Since when?"

The maid: "Since the first day I worked here. She always warns me about telling anything"

The maid added: "There is another dangerous thing"

King Jiff: "What is it?"

The maid: "She was pregnant a month ago; we helped her to get rid of the baby"

King Jiff: "Well, go"

King Jiff was very angry. He didn't know what he could do. He wanted to kill Ethan, however, he thought that his sister may do a bad thing.

Next day, King Jiff went to Lion who was getting better. King Jiff whispered to him laughing: "The girls missed you"

Lion said laughing: "I'll be fine very soon. Where is my family?"

King Jiff: "They're prisoners. I am waiting till you get better and then they would be judged"

After two weeks, Lion was recovered. He sat besides the king at the presence of his sister.

King Jiff ordered the guards to bring Lion's family. When they have been brought, he asked them: "Who did that with king's consultant and his sister husband?"

All of the presence was astonished. There was no answer. Hilton said: "Your Majesty, we don't know. We were all shocked when we saw him fallen to the ground on that case"

King Jiff: "Why did that whore said that Lion went to the palace when the guards asked her about him?"

July said angrily: "I was afraid. I don't know why I said that"

King Jiff: "You were afraid or you tried to escape of being punished for killing king's consultant and kinsman"

He added: "You don't want to tell the truth? I will give you a chance for 3 days. If you don't tell me the truth in 3 days, I'll judge you all to be killed"

While guards were leading the three friends to the prison, July said to Lion that she would tell the truth. The king wondered about the truth that July wanted to tell about.

Lion said that he did not know, however, he would tell him everything the next day.

Princess Kathy was angry; she asked King Jiff: "What did you say?"

King Jiff: "I'm your king; you have to obey my orders. You won't marry that raffish. I knew the truth"

Princess Kathy: "No, I don't mean that. I saw him accidently; it's the first time"

King Jiff pulled her hair and said: "I know that you meet him every week"

Princess Kathy went to her room crying and King Jiff went after her, she said: "I won't marry that short man"

King Jiff: "You will marry him. It's my last decision"

Princess Kathy: "Do you want to avenge me?"

King Jiff: "Consider it as you like to"

Princess Kathy: "I prefer death to marry this short guy"

King Jiff: "You will marry Lion next month"

King Jiff ordered the guards not to let her out of her room.

King Jiff returned back to Lion who asked: "Do you really want to make me marry Princess Kathy"

King Jiff: "Yes, I do. You're a complete man, aren't you?" then he continued: "you are just short, it doesn't lessen a man like you anything "

Lion: "I'm surprised by your decision"

King Jiff: "Are you happy?"

Lion: "Of course, I am. It's my honor to be the king's kinsman. Please, let me meet my family"

When he met them, July said: "You must help us or I will end up everything. It's all because of your fucking plan"

Hilton: "Are you crazy? Keep silent, let him think about a plan"

July: "It's my last decision. When we would be at the shearer place, I would tell the king about everything"

Lion: "Why? What did I do for you?"

July: "You have cheated us, you are unfaithful; you will marry king's sister"

Lion: "I swear, I did not know about this marriage but today"

Hilton: "Don't care about her bla bla; I'm sure that you're the right person who will save us"

Harry was crying, he said: "I'll say that I hit you because we were fighting together"

Hilton: "No, you would not bear the torture alone. We should survive together or die together"

Lion: "Well, I'll think about a way to get you out from here"

July: "Think about the issue, you bridegroom, or I'll tell the truth"

Lion went to the king who said: "Get ready, your wedding party would be held next month after I avenge who hurt you"

King Jiff added: "Don't you want to tell me what your mother wanted to say"

Lion: "Yes, I'll tell you the truth"

Lion began to tell the king a fake story, he said: "When I was there the last time, my mother said that she missed me and that she wanted me to stay with them. I agreed to stay, we were kidding and drinking. My father, Hilton went to bed and so did my brother, Harry. Then, my mother started crying; she complained from my father as he stopped loving her and he did not sleep with her for more than a year ago. She hugged me, looked at me and said that she wanted a man that love her strongly and kiss her fiercely. After that she began to hug and kiss me, besides, she tried to take my clothes off while I was trying to push her away from me. I said: 'I'm your son, please stop doing that, I'll tell my father'. However, I felt something hit my head when I was walking to my father's room. I did not want to say what happened, so that my father may kill her"

King Jiff: "Impossible! I cannot believe what I'm hearing. I should kill her myself. There is no woman that can do that with her son. She is a whore and a very bad mother. She deserves to be killed"

Lion tried to pretend crying: "Oh, Your Majesty, don't kill her, she is my mother, she was drunk"

King Jiff: "No, she is mine now, don't care for her again"

Lion: "Please, Your Majesty, I don't want my father to know about it. If you insist to kill her, promise me to do that secretly and without her knowledge in order not to say anything"

King Jiff: "I promise you that I would kill her secretly and without her knowledge"

After two weeks, king Jiff said to Lion that he would kill his mother secretly, he also said he feels sad for that but he swore to God that he would kill her. Lion pretended that he was crying pleading for the king to forgive her. However, Jiff stood up and said: "You're not the only person who lost his mother; you would forget her by time".

The next day, the guards suddenly entered the prison and asked for Jolly who asked: "what is happening?" they answered: "The king wants to see you".

224

They accompanied her to a room, and at the door they covered her eyes and said: "sit down". She sat down trembling; she did not know what was happening. When they get her head down, she shouted: "what is happening?", however, they cut her head in a moment.

The guard told the king that she has been executed. King Jiff said laughing: "Finally, your father will be happy for that"

Lion pretended that he was sad for killing Jolly. Jiff ordered the guards to get Hilton and Harry out of the prison and bring them to see the king. Lion was sitting down next to Kathy. Jiff said: "I forgive you as I knew who hurt king's consultant.

Hilton: "I don't understand what you mean. Where is my wife? I didn't see her since yesterday"

Jiff: "I did what you wanted to do"

Hilton fall down crying, he said: "Why did you kill my wife? She didn't hurt anyone"

Jiff: "I know that she who hurt Lion. I know it's a shock. Take that money and find another wife"

Hilton: "I don't want money, I want my wife. Who told you that she who hurt Lion?"

Jiff: "It's not your business. Take the money and go"

Hilton wiped his tears and said: "Could I bury her?"

Jiff: "We already buried her"

Hilton was very angry. He went home with Harry. He wanted to know why the king killed her. He was sure that Lion knew the reason.

225

A week after that, Lion went to see Hilton and Harry. Hilton said to him: "I know that you know everything. What did you say to the king? Why did you let them kill her?"

Lion: "Believe me, I don't know anything; she was sentenced to death secretly"

Hilton: "You're a liar. I'll kill him"

Lion: "Be prudent, I'll find you and Harry jobs in the palace. We'll live like kings"

Hilton shouted: "Did you forget the reason why we come to this land?"

Lion: "I did not forget, you who forgot that everything is burnt; weapons, missiles, the satellite, and everything; even our families are dead. We should live like the people on this land"

Lion continued: "Please, Hilton, Let us live and continue our lives here on this land. What do you want? Money, women, I will give you all what you need"

Hilton: "I don't want but to revenge for Jolly. Would you join us?"

Lion started crying:" No, I'm not with you. I want to make a family as all other people. I ever wished to marry and have children. There is no one could agree to let me marry his daughter, do you?"

Hilton: "Why not? You're a man"

Lion: "Don't cheat yourself. If you agree, your daughter won't. Think about that"

Lion looked to Harry: "And you Harry, it's our chance"

Hilton: "For me, I don't agree, but for Harry, he is free"

Harry: "What if I obeyed you, Hilton; what if we get out and made a war then defeated; we would be killed or become prisoners. I ... I will go with Lion. I want to live happily. War is not a good idea"

Hilton: "Then go with him. It's my problem"

Lion and Harry went to the palace. Lion entered alone to the king and said: "Do my Lord permit me to bring my brother in order to have a job and live here?"

Jiff was astonished, he said: "Your brother is welcomed, however, your father will live alone"

Lion: "He expelled my brother; he does not want anyone to live with him"

Jiff: "What a miserable man, how can he feel sad for an unfaithful wife?!"

Jiff added: "Well, let him sleep in guest room"

At dinner, Lion sat down next to Jiff and his sister while they were having their meal then he said: "My Lord, I want to tell you about a serious issue"

Jiff: "What is it?"

Lion looked to Kathy and stopped talking

Jiff said: "You can talk, Kathy is not a stranger, and she'll be your wife very soon"

Kathy stood up in order to leave, but Jiff spoke loudly to her saying: "Stop Kathy. Sit down and listen to your husband"

Kathy sat down then Lion said: "My father is very angry because you have killed my mother. I'm afraid he may do something wrong. I'm not responsible for what he may do"

Jiff: "Do you want to put him in the prison again?"

Lion: "No, your majesty, just let more guards accompany him and don't let him go out of his house"

Early in the morning next day, the king sent 4 guards to stay at Hilton house's gate. When Hilton wanted to go out, the guards prevented him and told him that the king ordered not to let him go out, instead, they should bring him whatever he wants. Hilton was very angry, although he continued digging he found himself a way out of the empire's walls, he ran to where they hid the weapons and he get all weapons and put them under his house to be easy to take anything whenever he wants , he asked to see Lion immediately, however, they told him that he cannot meet or speak to anyone.

Hilton: "Well, we'll see who is the looser"

The king made Harry a supervisor of the stable; he was assigned to prepare the horses for the king. Lion tried to change that job, however, Jiff refused saying that there is no other job. Harry was shocked when he knew about his job; he thought he would be a respectable employee who works in a high position. Lion told him that he would try to convince the king that Harry deserved a better job. He also tried to persuade Harry that the king needed horses scarcely, so there was no problem with working as a stable supervisor; "you would stay without work most of the time". Harry was convinced to accept the job provided that Lion would seek another suitable job.

Lion and Kathy's marriage approached, the king ordered to prepare a suitable wedding party that would be held in the square. People were invited to the party. The high-class were invited to attend in the palace. Lion was preparing himself for the party when Harry asked him about Hilton. Lion was very worried; he stressed guards on Hilton lest he would spoil his party.

Harry said: "Did you forget to invite Hilton?"

Lion: "Impossible! I'm afraid that he may spoil the wedding party"

Harry: "How could he do? He is a prisoner now. Please, Lion, invite him"

Lion agreed to invite Hilton provided that he should be inspected well before entering the place.

On the wedding day, the king was sitting on the throne; his sister was on the right while Lion was on the left of the throne. The high-class people attended to congratulate the couple. Kathy was unhappy; she was very sad because she haven't married her beloved one. She wished if she could escape from the palace in order to marry Ethan.

Hilton attended the party and greeted the couple. At the middle of the party, Hilton went to the throne and asked for permission to give his son a present. Jiff agreed saying: "No problem, what is your present?"

Hilton got out a grenade from his pocket. When Lion saw the grenade, he shook his head for Hilton expressing: "No, don't do that"

Jiff smiled to Hilton who was catching the grenade while his finger was upon the safety valve in order to pull it as soon as he gives the bomb to the king.

Hilton pull the safety valve while Lion stood up, he wanted to shout for Hilton to prevent him from doing that. King Jiff asked: "What is this?" while Lion said: "No, no, no", he hugged his wife, Kathy and threw her on the ground and suddenly, the bomb exploded at the king. People cried and the guards killed Hilton. Kathy cried: "Brother, brother". She hurried to see him but his body was cut into shreds. When Harry saw the accident he escaped to their house crying for Hilton's death. He wished if he was killed, too. Harry was afraid of killing Lion, as Lion was the only person who remained from his friends.

Kathy was shocked, she had breakdown. Lion stayed at her room till she regained her consciousness. When she saw Lion, she began to cry: "Why did you kill my brother?"

Lion: "I did not kill him"

Kathy: "The killer is your father"

Lion: "You know that he is not my father. He wanted to revenge for my mother"

Kathy: "What was he holding in his hand? Why did you shout and throw me to the ground when you saw your father getting it from his pocket?"

Lion: "I swear I don't know what is it. I just felt that it was something dangerous"

Kathy said to the guards: "Well, take him to the prison until he tells me the truth"

The guards took him to prison while he was shouting: "I'm your husband, I saved your life. If I want to kill you, I never would save you"

The guards pulling Lion in prison. He was saying: "why did you do that, Hilton. What had you benefit from doing that? We would all die?"

After two days, Harry entered to the prison; Lion was astonished, he asked him: "Why did you come back"

Harry: "I miss that place, and I don't want to leave you alone. I come here to turn myself in. when the queen asked me about what I know, I told her that I don't know anything then she ordered to put me in prison with you"

Lion: "Why didn't you escape, or why didn't you do like what Hilton did in order to end up all that?"

Harry: "Death is our fate. I was about to die when we landed on this land; however, it was not my fate day. Now, I live the same experience again"

After some days, the guards took them to the queen who said: "The guards searched your father's house ..."

Lion: "He is not our father. We are not responsible for what he did"

Kathy: "Just listen and don't disturb me. The guards found a hole which was dug to be attached to the outside of the city. From where did he bring the grenades?"

Lion: "We don't know. He may found them or even made them. He expelled us and we live here a long time ago. He told us that he is not our father"

Kathy: "Who invited him to the party?"

Lion: "I invited him because he is like my father. I ordered the guards to inspect him well and they did not find anything dangerous.

Naturally, the guards don't let any armed person to get in the palace"

Kathy: "Yes, no armed one can enter here"

Kathy continued: "I won't judge you, do you accept a fair judgment?"

Lion and Harry: "Yes, we do"

Kathy: "I will choose some wise people in order to judge you. I won't be unjust like my brother. I will be fair"

Lion: "I'm your husband"

Kathy shouted: "You're not my husband. Marriage is conditioned to acceptance. I did not agree to marry you; however, my brother compelled me"

Kathy added: "You would be judged in a few days"

In the prison, Lion and Harry agreed to say typical answers. At the court, they were four persons who should judge them. The four persons asked Lion and Harry: "Do you agree that we judge you?"

Lion and Harry: "Yes, we do"

The judges asked Kathy: "Your Majesty, do you agree that we judge between you and them?"

Kathy: "Yes, I do"

The judges started asking the two parties. Lion and Harry were composing stories about their parents as King Jiff knew before. After weeks of investigations, the judges said that Lion and Harry are not guilty. They said that Hilton's action was a revenge for his wife killing while the children did not share in the crime.

When Lion and Harry became free, Kathy said that she did not want to see them. However, days after, Queen Kathy called Lion and asked him to divorce her. Lion refused although she offered him money. There was a rule in the empire that only man can divorces his wife by declaring for people that he has divorced her voluntarily so that she can marry another person, in return, a husband should take half of the heritage or a wife cannot get married to any other person.

Kathy tried a lot to persuade him to divorce her, however, he didn't agree because he loved her. At last, he knew that it was impossible for Kathy to accept him as a husband, so he agreed to divorce her. Kathy told him that she would give him whatever he would ask for.

Lion thought about what he should take in return to divorce. He asked to govern the empire; Lion said: "I want to be the viceroy of the Empire"

Kathy: "Are you crazy?"

Lion said: "Then, we don't agree" and then he went out.

Kathy was nervous thinking about her life. She didn't find any way out but to accept his request.

Kathy thought: "What would happen if he became the viceroy. Well, I'll find a way to get rid of him"

After two days, Kathy sent to Lion to tell him that she agreed to his condition. Lion said: "Well, now we agree. Declare that for people and then I would declare that I have divorced you"

Lion already declared that he has divorced Kathy after she has declared that Lion became the viceroy of the Empire. Few Days after that, Kathy was married to Ethan, her beloved one, whom she always sacrificed for. She assigned him as her advisor and Lion assigned Harry as his advisor, too.

Ethan started to annoy Lion then wonder about the reason of assigning Lion as a viceroy while he is just a consultant; "Why he is the viceroy while I'm a consultant; I'm your husband and beloved"

Kathy: "My beloved helps me a lot and I'm happy that he works with me. Why are you annoyed?"

Ethan: "I who deserve to be the viceroy, not him"

Kathy: "If I did not make him the viceroy, I would not have married you"

Ethan: "You should find a way to make me the viceroy instead of him; you are the queen, you who give orders"

Ethan continued: "What if that short man became the king of the Empire after a long time? Then, I would be a servant in the palace. My dear, think about our coming life and the future of our children, too"

Kathy: "I promise you that I would get rid of him, but not now. Hug me, please. You always say that when we marry, we won't get out of our room"

The Empire was in its best period after King Jiff's death as Lion was doing well and governs justly unlike Jiff.

Every day, Ethan was discussing with Kathy about Lion and his position. He did not stop talking about that issue till Kathy became angry. She confirmed that she would ensure their future; "He is doing very well, and that makes me free in order to care for you all the time. He solves the problems of the Empire without my help and he did not do any mistake, what can I punish him for?"

Kathy added: "Did you marry me for governance?"

Ethan: "No, I married you because I love you; I'm ready to live with you anywhere; even in a small house. However, I want to help you; I'm your husband and I deserve that, not him"

Kathy hugged Ethan and said: "Ethan, don't bother with the Empire. I'm here only for you"

One day, Harry hurried to Lion to tell him that he saw some spaceships behind the palace and that their spaceship was there, too. Harry said: "that means that they have captured all spaceships landed on their land"

Lion: "So, what?"

Harry: "We should find a way in order to contact with Earth so as to tell them what happens"

Lion: "No, we should not do that. If they know the truth about us, we would be killed"

Harry became angry with Lion, he said: "Have you changed your mind after you became the Viceroy?"

Lion: "I did not change my mind; however, there is no other way"

Harry: "Don't say that; we haven't tried yet. We should do our best before we resign to our fate"

Lion: "I'm afraid"

Harry: "of what? You're the governor of this empire and the queen is busy with his beloved husband. Please, it's our last chance"

Lion: "Let me think about the issue"

Harry: "Well, you should find a way next week"

Then he continued: "No, you should decide tomorrow. Do you think the queen would keep you the viceroy while her husband has no authority in their land? Look at him to know how he malice you"

Lion: "I knew that the queen will make him the army commander"

Harry: "Today he is an army commander and tomorrow he would be a viceroy and then we would be out of the palace"

Lion: "Well, let me think about the matter"

Days passed, Harry went to the first spaceship and searched in it, and then he searched the second spaceship, too. After that, he went to their spaceship which was burnt badly. He began to search in the good part where he found the books whose sheets were crust and stuck to each other because of water. Harry took the books and hurried to the palace, however, Ethan noticed. When Ethan asked him about the books, Harry began stuttering; he said: "They are mine; they fall into the water so I put them out side in order to dry"

Ethan: "Well"

Harry went to his room and tried to open the sheets of the books. The sheets were stuck to each other and some written words disappeared. Harry separated the stuck sheets and stayed one week reading them till he knew that there is a wireless device in the spaceship. Next day, Harry went to the spaceship in order to look for the device which he found in the control room. Harry hurried to Lion and told him that he found a way.

Lion: "What is it?"

Harry: "I found a wireless device in our room"

Lion: "Do you forget that there is a burnt satellite?"

Harry was disappointed when he knew that. He begged Lion asking for his permission to try for the last time. Lion said: "Well, just one trial. Be careful of being noticed"

Harry: "If any one saw me, I'll say I just have a look"

The next day, Harry tried to turn the device on, but to no avail. He took it to the second spaceship and tried one more, but to no avail, too. Most of the second spaceship was burnt. Harry tried to turn on the power of the first spaceship; however it did not work, too. Harry went down to search for the reason of the damage. He found two expired batteries, and then he went to the second spaceship where he found a valid battery. He tried to remove it, but he could not. Harry searched for a screw in order to use it to remove the battery. He found some screws by which he removed the battery. Harry took the battery to the first spaceship and connected wires of the call device. The control room began to work and Harry tried calling Earth: "Hello, hello, do you hear me?" But he did not find any answer, he stopped trying intending to retry the next day.

Next day, Harry tried to call Earth again. Every trial, he waited for 5 minutes supposedly he receive any signal, but to no avail. Every day he repeated: "Hello, from the new land, do you hear me?"

One day, Ethan saw him going out, he watched him till he saw him doing that every day. Ethan followed him till he saw him entering the first spaceship. Ethan listened to him saying: "Hello, hello, do you hear me? We are in the new land"

Ethan hurried to the queen and told her that Harry is in the evil bearer. Ethan told her that he heard Harry as if he was speaking to somebody saying: "Hello, do you hear me? We're in the new land". The queen took some soldiers and hurried to the spaceship. Lion saw them they were in a hurry; he thought they caught Harry in the spaceship, so he followed them.

The queen asked: "What is this? What are you doing here?"

Harry began stuttering: "Nothing, I was just playing here"

The Queen shouted: "Whom you speaking to?"

Harry: "I swear, I was speaking to myself"

Suddenly, they heard: "Sh... Sh... Yes, we hear you clearly"

The Queen caught him from his hair and put a sward on his neck and said: "Tell them not to come here or they would be killed. Tell them that all who came here have been killed and that you have been captured in order to convey this message. Tell them also that this is our land and we won't let any stranger live here"

Harry conveyed the message then the queen killed him with the sward.

Lion entered and saw what happened. Harry was gasping for breath. The queen ordered the guards to put Lion in prison and burn all the spaceships.

In the prison, Lion admitted everything. He was accused of treason and was sentenced to death.

Before his death, Lion stood while people were throwing stones and rubbish on him. He said: "I have never lived in my land; however I lived on this land the happiest life although it was very short. I wish if I was able to live my whole life here, however, it's my fate"

Lion's head has been cut and hanged in the square for one week.

Do the attacks would happen again?

You will know that when you read the 2nd. Part of this story;
    'Struggle on lands'

By. Waheed alghslan

@Waheed_alghslan

www.ingramcontent.com/pod-product-compliance
Lightning Source LLC
Chambersburg PA
CBHW071150170626
46809CB00002B/847